Foreword

Ian Williams, the artist who defies conventional explanation. In the 15 years or so that I have known Ian, I have learned two things for certain. Ian is an artist who defies conventional classification. And when he puts his personal drive and inspiration into a new field of activity, he generally succeeds.

There is another aspect, too. He manages to do all this without excluding people from his life. He's always welcoming, always chatty, always involved. He's part of his community wherever he is based, often quite a leading part. So exactly when he's got time to write, to develop ceramist skills, to paint, to create poetry, to organise charity events — and to overcome the tides of vicissitudes which have come at him from all angles — is really a mystery.

Decades back now, the artist Ian emerged from a police officer who got involved in art therapy as part of his recovery from a major set of injuries incurred in the line of duty. Now art therapy is used on all sorts of people without them even remotely turning into actual artists — let alone artists who can work successfully in a variety of disciplines.

But it never seems to occur to Ian that whatever he is trying will not work — and he does not achieve that by hiding his ventures from the public. Not at all. Each new artistic excursion is thrown open to the public to be tested in the harsh court of public opinion and the marketplace.

Ian Williams is an extraordinary example of the pure power of imagination and a rare ability to connect that imagination to a really wide range of ways of expressing it.

Welcome to his world!

Fred Silver
Editor of The Skye Magazine

INCANDESCENT LIGHT

Chapter 1
The Beginning

Time, space and balance have always been so, as, without balance, time and space were unstable. Conscience then came into existence.

Conscience was an entity which on the planet Earth many referred to as *God*. In other civilisations throughout the universes, this entity has many and varied names.

I shall refer to this entity as *The Other*. The Other is pure and is known for it's omniscient and benevolence. It could be in many places throughout the universes and take on any form without thought.

Following The Other there were several other entities; they also possessed great power and will, however not the full power of The Other. They are known as *The Firsts*, but who are in fact, lesser Gods.

Lesser does not exactly express their real status within the universes, time and space, as between The Firsts they had many and complex inter-universe tasks to both study and resolve. Balance must be safeguarded. However, even with their great, almost omnipotent powers, futures were never fully disclosed.

Hints and possibilities only became clearer as time, space and balance allowed.

Clarity too soon could put balance in jeopardy.

Chapter 2
Greed

While several of The Firsts were consumed with studying the nature of the universes, The Other investigated its contents whilst keeping an eagle eye on The Firsts.

The Other discovered that The Firsts were not, in fact, the only other entities present.

The evidence suggested that although faint, other entities were existing, coming into being and that this process would continue for all time. One entity, in particular, appeared to be the complete opposite of The Other and The Firsts. This entity did not possess the same power as The Other but had powers that equalled The Firsts. This entity required close observations and monitoring. In time this entity would have many and varied names including, Lucifer, Satan, Devil and Greed. I will refer to it as *Greed.*

Chapter 3
Chaos and Patience

Several more entities came into being, two of these being Chaos and Patience. The Other recognised them and began to guide them in their roles; they became more akin to brothers.

There were several more entities, their future and time frames were not clear, but The Other could sense them and their importance; they would be nurtured and hidden until the time was appropriate. Until this time, The Other would shield their existence from all; however hints of their existence were there. This is balance.

And so, the struggle between good and evil began.

Chapter 4
Chaos and Greed

Chaos is powerful and essential. For this reason, Greed wanted to consume Chaos. The result would give Greed more power than The Other. Greed could also sense the presence of other entities; however their identities were not clear by any means and so Greed went to where Chaos was, ignoring all else for the time being. Greed's abilities to seduce and deceive are overwhelming.

Its will could locate and capitalise on any weakness. As the two entities moved slowly together and travelled in the same direction, The Other became only too aware of the unholy union beginning to collide. Chaos was unwittingly allowing Greed to absorb its power and will; it was powerless to respond as Greed grew stronger.

Chapter 5
Seduction

The seduction and the alliance of the two great powers of Greed and Chaos got closer. The elements contained within the universes started to agitate and boil. Solar systems that had been neighbours collided and burned. Galaxy after galaxy shifted uncomfortably in opposite directions.

Greed swelled and its influence on Chaos was almost complete. The merging began. Then in an instant, entrapment.

Chaos was imprisoned, its powers absorbed by Greed, the seduction was now done. Greed exalted in its completed trap; focusing on itself, it dropped its guard.

Chapter 6
Imprisonment

The Other had to respond as the instability of time and space was in peril. However, as everything is related and it is forbidden to completely destroy and unmake anything, The Other gathered its will, with a single focused thought and in the instant that Greed allowed its guard down The Other executed its full force.

All of the time and space surrounding Greed suddenly exploded. Every atom and element heated and started to reform. Surrounded on every possible side, even through time, Greed was snared. Iron formed most of the matter, which now prevented Greed's escape. The Other knew that iron was able to curtail evil intent. More atoms joined with the iron, pressure started to build around Greed, and its prisoner Chaos, the mass of iron shimmered into a globe, eventually becoming Earth

Very soon, a sphere of boiling gasses had completely enrobed Greed. The newly formed Earth began to travel towards a new star—the sun, its gravitational pull overwhelming it. On its journey, more atoms joined; this had the effect of further entombing Greed and Chaos. More pressure was exerted when other more liquid atoms surrounded the Earth, wrapping around the hard iron cell.

Travelling vast distances, the Earth eventually slowed and went into an orbit around the sun. Enraged and weaker but still possessing great power, Greed summoned its will. Locating a nearby asteroid Greed forced it to alter its celestial course, hoping that it would collide with the Earth. The intention was to smash open the core of the earth and escape. The asteroid connected with the Earth, but without sufficient energy or power, neither did Greed have enough power of will. The impact was not sufficient to allow their escape.

The result was the birth of a small moon that would in time, accompany the new planet Earth. The exertion of such power and energy rendered Greed and Chaos temporarily dormant. Millions of Earth years passed, evolution continued. But slowly and surely, the prisoners started to reawaken.

Chapter 7
Seeds

In all of the universes, there are only a few planets where life can be sustained and thrive. They are so rare and special that The Other watches them very carefully, guarding the precious worlds.

In particular, the planet Earth, this is where The Other chose to deliver and secrete several more seed entities. Even with the prisoners held captive there.

Chapter 8
Dark Water

Silently as the essences of Greed and Chaos began to get stronger in the time of the prehistoric animals, the killing spread, 'dog eat dog'. The essence and soul of each slaughtered creature found its way to feed Greed. For it knew that its strength was returning and of course what Greed wanted he took.

Suffering made the soul that much more pleasing. And so Greed silently placed within the minds of the giants a need to spread hurt and unnecessary suffering. The waters began to blacken with the filth of Greed; the time approached when Greed's strength was beginning to overwhelm.

Escape was within its grasp. It was at this point that The Other again intervened, locating a tiny saltwater comet and sending it to collide with the Earth. Contained within this comet was concentrated salt ice water; on impact, the ice water melted and quickly dispersed. Salt was essential to prevent evil from escaping. There was now enough pressure once again to incarcerate Greed. There was a heavy and regrettable toll in creating this grave act.

It brought about the end of the giant animals and the extinction of many life forms.

However, within the new water were the building blocks of a new and stronger life-form—mankind. Embedded in mankind was Strength.

Chapter 9
Strength

In time Earth started to heal. New life grew. The evolution of this small and precious planet began. A blue and green gem travelling around its star. Time passed and Earth left it's infancy, growing and maturing. Slowly, quietly out of sight of all else apart from The Other, Strength began to evolve, gaining consciousness and purpose.

And so began a new era on a single huge continent.

Chapter 10
Escape

S uch was the renewed power following further incarceration, Greed as always accompanied by Chaos was once again able to reach out from the core of Earth.

Exuding pressure and influence from deep within, Greed was able to reach with evil tendrils the softer and outer areas of the planet until the large landmass started to crack, allowing more access. Outwardly it seemed that the planet was adjusting and developing at its own pace.

Great continental plates fractured, forming new continents, the fractures opened up gigantic volcanic action; this action served Greed's purpose as it acted like a smokescreen. To Greed, this was perfection. Millions of human years passed, a plan was being formed. Greed was again sensing other possibilities. But even with all that was taking place, the noise and destruction, balance continued, assisting Strength to evolve unnoticed.

Chapter 11
Peter

Surrounded by clear aquamarine waters, the Isle of Minzo lies in the centre of the Sea of Days. The island is the summit of a gigantic mountain; the sides of the mountain descend miles under the water into a very dark world.

The depth of the water separates what resides in the dark from the aquamarine beauty of the clear waters surrounding Minzo.

Legend, however, tells of incidents in the long distant past when lines were crossed and darkness ascended; death and misery followed.

"Mum, I have to repair the boat before I gather the fish!"

Peter was a boy of 13 years of age. He lived with his mother, Pearl and his younger sister, Joy. Peter was a slightly built boy; however, his size hid his inner-strength and will. He became the family provider following the loss of his father, David, who one day, as usual, six years ago, went out to fish and never returned. His boat Aurora was found days later abandoned in calm waters.

When his boat was located, all of his equipment was intact. It had not been used. The thing that puzzled those who found Aurora was a smell, the strong smell of sulphur hung in the air. Presumed lost forever, a brief service took place on the shoreline.

Bryn the village elder made special note as to David's qualities both as a loving husband and devoted father. The loss of David to his family and the community was grave. Wildflower petals were placed onto the surface of the sea; the hope was that one day they might reunite.

Following the service, it was custom for Peter to become the 'Man' of the house.

"Peter, you will join your sister and me to eat before you continue to repair the boat." *"YES*, Mum." Supper consisted of several small sweet-fleshed fish and home-grown vegetables. Pearl had baked a corn loaf. Before eating, Peter said some words: "We thank you for our food and ask for safe fishing."

For reasons not clear to Peter, when he said his words, he felt somehow close to his lost father David, and in his mind, he could see light; a light so bright he had to put his mind's hand over his mind's eyes. He also thought he could hear soft whispers but could not make out what the words said and when he thought about the whispering, he lost track of what he was thinking about.

During the meal, Pearl looked closely at her son. She loved Peter. It hurt her heart, a boy so young with heavy responsibilities; a boy who became a man when his father was lost, but a boy all the same. Pearl looked into his soft brown eyes and saw the inner-strength she had seen take her son from boyhood into a young man.

Pearl also knew that her daughter Joy loved her older brother and had become ever closer to him following the loss of their father. Dinner finished, Joy took the dishes and washed them. Peter lifted his bag of tools, said his goodbyes, and left for the boat. The walk to the boat took only minutes. Peter looked back for a second to the small fishing croft in which he lived with his family; a white-washed small home with two windows to the front and a red roof. The rest of the village spread longways and backwards; the school was set almost in the centre of the village. It was a happy village where the community shared responsibilities and helped each other when help was needed. The loss of David was felt by so many; they cared for Pearl and her family. Special care was given by the village elder, Bryn.

Bryn was a kind man who took his role seriously and with great pride, and the community liked and respected him. And so the village continued its usual path, for now.

Chapter 12
Aurora

Peter walked slowly down to the seashore. The sun felt warm on his back, and he was happy; he thought about his family and the love he had for his mother and sister; he thought about his father. It was at this moment he thought he could hear voices talking in soft tones. Looking around himself, nobody was to be seen.

"But I heard someone!" he said aloud to himself. Feeling slightly foolish that he had talked out loud to himself, he continued to walk the relatively short distance to where his boat sat on the stoney seashore. The water slowly pushed up the slight incline of the shore, breaking on the stones. It was a sound that comforted Peter. He had listened to this sound for as long as he could remember; it made him feel happy.

Sitting proud upon the pebbles was his boat Aurora, a wooden clinker-built fishing boat with an open deck and large white sail. The hull was painted soft blue with white detail. Peter had inherited the boat following the loss of his father. Peter was so proud of the boat; it was the tool for him to feed his family; he knew the boat, it was his friend, and he tended the boat with fondness. The memories of happy times sailing, fishing, and having fun with his father almost brought a tear to his eye, only to be replaced with a brightness and an unconscious knowledge that he had a task and that Aurora was part of this task. The moment passed, and he got to work on the boat, corking the boards and sealing the gaps between them. He had watched his father doing exactly this job, placing the wick cord up to the gap and tapping it into the exposed area, creating a seal.

Time passed so quickly as he worked; he so enjoyed the work it was almost hard to put down the tools and return to his home, where his mother waited for him. Following dinner, Peter took himself to his bed, where he soon slipped into sleep.

Chapter 13
Awakening

Peter had known about The Other ever since he knew how to think and remember; he was unsure how long, but it seemed forever. He could not talk about The Other as when the thoughts came to the front of his mind; they were quickly replaced with other, not so important memories and thoughts. Tonight, however, there was something different. Was he still sleeping, or was this real? Peter was standing in a place where he felt completely safe and felt the sense of overwhelming love; he was happy in this place, it seemed familiar, but he simply could not place it. Then in his mind, he was aware of The Other.

"Yes, Peter, it is me. You have known me for a long, long time. I have known you forever. You will know me more soon; you have a task so important the result will last for a millennium. I will guide you; however, it will be your choice." Peter woke up warm in his bed, not knowing how significant that night had been; he was aware that he had something on his mind but not what. Getting washed and dressed, then walking into the small and homely kitchen, he was greeted by Pearl, his mother. Pearl took a second look at her son; she saw something only a loving mother could see, a change, a subtle change

Somehow overnight, he had begun the journey from boyhood into manhood, but there was something more that Pearl could not quite understand, and when she thought about this alteration, her mind went to thinking about the steaming porridge slowly bubbling on the stove, all other thoughts and concerns hidden in the edges of her mind. Pearl hummed her favourite melody as she carefully stirred the warm creamy breakfast. Peter noticed the look from his mother and said, "I love you, mum". As he said it, he felt the warmest feeling deep in his body, a feeling he briefly recalled from his sleep the previous night. Pearl said, "And I love you, son." Pearl turned to attend to breakfast, a tear falling from her eye.

Having completed the work on his boat, Peter began to prepare his nets and bait as he was to go fishing the following day. He enjoyed sitting on an upturned box, slowly and precisely examining the nets for damage before repairing them. He had spent many hours sitting next to his father, watching closely how to repair the nets. All the time, his father would tell Peter stories of years gone by, of the big fish that 'simply got away!' Peter loved listening to the stories; he longed for the time when he, too, would set sail and catch the fish they needed. With a sigh of regret, he thought about his father and how much he missed him and his stories; now it was Peter who recounted the stories to himself. A brief smile touched his lips, and he continued to repair the nets. Peter was a competent fisherman: he could read the weather and the signs presenting themselves as to the location of the fish, he seemed to possess the knack for being in the right place at the right time, and he always presented a healthy catch on his return, always to the delight of his mother and sister. Supper that evening was simple, cornbread and several small tasty fish and vegetables grown by his mother. With a comfortably full stomach, Peter said good night to his sister and mother and went to his bed—he was preparing for an early start the next morning.

He fell to sleep straight away. Deep in his slumber, he

found himself in that place where he was happy and felt the overwhelming sense of love, and then he was aware of The Other. "Welcome, Peter," he heard, or was the voice in his mind? Peter looked about himself; he did not see anyone but was aware that he was not alone; a brief chill touched his heart. "Peter, I am with you, I always have been, you have nothing to fear in this place, it is yours, it is your safe haven, so learn to love this place and to trust in it for should you ever need to be here you just need to think it, and you will be here." Peter was alone again but very contented. His sleep continued uneventfully apart from one moment when he thought he could smell the unmistakable odour of rotting eggs.

The smell vanished as quickly as it had arrived.

Chapter 14
Sulphur

Waking at first light the following day, Peter dressed and quietly went downstairs to collect his food for the day before leaving for the shore. Waiting for him at the kitchen table was Pearl, his mother. "Mum, you are up early," Peter said.

"Yes, I could not rest, and I wanted to walk with you to the shore. I would walk with your father in the mornings before he set sail and enjoyed the scent from the sea, mixing with the beautiful wildflower aroma. It always made the start of a day so special. Shall we go then?" Pearl said softly but with authority.

The air was heavy with the scent of wildflowers, punctuated with the fresh salty smell of the sea. Taking in a huge breath, Pearl filled her lungs with the joyful air; her heart soared. "Better than that awful rotten egg smell during the night," she half said to herself. Sending an enquiring look at his mother, Peter said, "You smelled it too?"

On the horizon, the sun began to rise, the deep orange glowing on all of the surfaces facing it. The sky seemed to shimmer with happiness whilst the sea quietly reflected the sunrise, without a cloud in the sky and with the hint of a breeze coming offshore. Peter said, "Should be a good day for fishing. I can feel it in my bones."

Pearl gently smiled and ruffled Peter's hair. "Your father would say the same thing." Pearl gently took Peter's face in her soft but strong hands. She looked directly into his eyes and said, "Peter, you will be careful, won't you? When you have enough catch,

26

return, and I will cook you a feast of the 'catch of the day'. Peter gently pulled his head away. He was a man now, or so he thought; however, deep down, he wanted to stay in his mother's grasp forever. "Yes, mum, of course, I will. I would not miss your feast for anything. I love you."

Arriving at his boat, Aurora, Peter quickly readied her. With the help of Pearl, they gently pushed the boat down the slight incline, the small rounded stones making the journey into the clear aquamarine waters a little easier, the gentle offshore breeze building slightly, which assisted their efforts. Peter jumped aboard and pulled the sail rope; with ease, the small sail ascended, quickly filling with the breeze.

Aurora silently slipped into the water, leaving the shore behind. Pearl stood ankle-deep in the warm water, unconsciously massaging the soles of her feet on the warm, rounded pebbles, and she raised her gentle hand and waved to her son. "Please bring him safely home," she said to herself. Pearl watched as Peter sailed his boat confidently out into the calm waters, being aided by the offshore breeze. Soon he was almost out of sight.

Pearl turned and began to walk up the shore back to her home. The sun continued to rise, it's warmth touching the slender shoulders of Pearl, comforting her; this made Pearl smile. As Pearl approached her home, a sudden sharp shard of wind blew. The strange thing she realised was that the wind came from her back, from the sea where only a short time ago the breeze was going offshore. This sharp gust also carried with it something familiar; it made Pearl shudder, as with a retching feeling in her soul, she smelled rotten eggs, sulphur. Pearl spun around and looked out to sea. There was no sign of Aurora. The sun continued to rise, and the aquamarine sea looked calm and inviting. "It must have been my imagination," she said to herself. There was no more nasty smell and the breeze once again gently moved the sweet fragrant air around her. Pearl went indoors and continued her day. In the depth of her mind, however, Pearl had an uncomfortable feeling, an intuition that only mothers have about their children—she sensed danger.

Chapter 15
Silence

Peter sailed Aurora further out to sea. With the forward motion of the boat came the sweet fresh sea-salty air into his face, filling his lungs. Together with the warmth of the sun on his face, it felt so good. "This is going to be a good day," Peter said to himself. Peter turned his boat into the breeze and let the sail down. Aurora came to a silent stop. The sound of lapping water was the only sound to be heard. Peter set his nets ready to enter the water then let them go. With the boat moving slowly in the breeze, the nets gently entered the water, vanishing below the surface. The nets were suspended on the surface by a series of small floats, and Peter would watch the floats until they detected movement; then, he would have a good idea if the nets had done the job of catching the fish

Peter sat waiting for any movement, but nothing came. He found it rather strange that there was no movement at all. He also realised that there was no other sound coming from around him. He would usually hear gulls chattering and calling to each other, waiting just above him with eager anticipation for the end of the catch, or even hear a distant splash, the sound of a dolphin breaching in the water, but nothing today.

Chapter 16
Patience

From high above the planet, being carried on the thinnest of air, Patience continued its earthly vigil, observing the changes and the progress taking place, waiting for a moment in everlasting time when an event so significant was to take place—observing the evolution of mankind, waiting for Strength to come of age. As time has no meaning, Strength was slightly surprised by how quickly mankind evolved. Expecting this fresh, new, unique entity to take a slower path to where they were now. It seemed, however, that evolution had different ideas.

As a basic 'being', the need to satisfy the hunger for all things within mankind meant that they began to think about more than simply the chase. They evolved into hunters; they applied thought as to the question of how to use less energy to secure the same hunting success. They easily developed cunning, stealth, and the realisation that man had one facility that they alone controlled—fire. This was to change the road they travelled—fire was power. Mankind was power, and they used this newfound power, not just for the food they needed but for other matters: desire and want.

It was clear that even entombed and locked in the the very core of the planet, Greed was able somehow to use its influence on this fast-paced evolution. The genie was out of the bottle; the once subtle and silent evolution of man was forever over. Man was formidable, smart, and developing at such a pace that it was not easy to monitor. Patience had concerns but was confident that mankind would come to no harm. This confidence was misplaced.

As time continued, man learned more and gained knowledge; with this knowledge came power, with more power came the desire for more. Sensing the desires of man, Greed's dark tendrils found ways to penetrate the finest fissures in the core of the planet, creeping slowly, silently, without notice but surely through the outer layers of the planet, then as micro bubbles into the oceans and seas, arriving as vapour, the foulest vapour, a sulphurous nostril attacking odour; its intention, to corrupt those willing to accept its will.

Power and desire are a dangerous combination; one drives the other. The consequences are too terrible to comprehend. The sadness and disquiet can last forever.

Almost from the time that man learned to stand, he felt he towered over all others, including his fellow man, with grotesque, vile consequences. From time to time individuals of particular evil intent came into being; their intention was to dominate all others. Nothing would stop their need for power; nothing would halt the ravenous hunger, the blinding thirst of desire.

It was during this time that millions of human beings could be heard to scream in terror, shudder in disbelief that their neighbour could act in such an inhuman way; millions were slaughtered at the will of those handfuls of Greed's disciples. Between them, death and destruction and desire ruled almost without challenge. The rancid stench of Greed was influencing areas all over the planet; its power was building, influencing the weak-willed, the wicked blinkered ones who were so feared and held no regard for others.

During this period, Greed sensed a familiar but strangely different entity, different to the other entities known to Greed, but it was powerful and dangerous. However powerful if Greed could possess it, then nothing could stand in its way, nothing. The search for Peter and his family started. With cunning and determination to remain out of sight, a plan was hatched.

Chapter 17
Calm Water

Peter began to haul in his nets. As the weight of the nets left the water, so his boat Aurora picked up pace on the surface of the water. The breeze seemed to be picking up. Peter quickly landed the empty nets onto the deck of the boat. He was surprised to see a white water bow wave. He thought, "How is this possible? I don't even have my sail up!" His boat was travelling at quite a pace. Peter hauled the sail to steady his vessel, the wind filled his sails, and Aurora cut through the relative calm water. A brief chill ran through Peter; this was overtaken by excitement as he sailed his boat at such a speed, and to add to his excitement was what he could see in the distance. It seemed that the whole of the sea in his path was boiling with fish at the surface. Peter placed the tiller firmly and raced to the apparent bonanza of fish.

Chapter 18
Tsunami

Matters were moving at such a pace; the plan was working, the trap was set in place, the bait had been taken. Something, however, was not right. Patience was irritatingly close, constantly watching. Greed began to produce a diversion; it was simple, get rid of Patience and isolate the boy.

Sending terrible tendril-like fingers through the seabed, Greed found what he searched for; on the other side of the planet, deep under the water, the dreadful fingers found the fault line in an underwater mountain range, a remnant from the devastation many centuries earlier. There the fingers located the pressure points lying deep in the rocks, and with little effort of its will, Greed opened a minor pressure point. In an instant, the small crack became larger, travelling at countless tens of miles a second, then with a scream of agony, the seabed snapped along the fault line.

A whiplash effect pushed a gigantic wall of seabed upwards hundreds of feet; this, in turn, pushed the sea up. The energy released was massive. A wave grew and grew and began to travel at high speed towards land; nothing in its path was safe, nothing in its path could withstand the power. Within a short time, the wave landed. Screams of terror rang out as hundreds of thousands of people shared a single fear—death.

From the other side of the planet, Patience heard the seabed crack, heard the cries, and felt the overwhelming feeling of death. On invisible jet stream winds, Patience flew towards the unimaginable scenes of devastation.

Mother Earth, herself, shuddered at the heartache; it was too late for action, the deed was done. Terror and death filled the air.

The Other was the first to shed a tear at the scene.

Chapter 19
The Trap

It was at this moment that the real horror struck Patience, sensing that Peter was not approaching the catch of the day but a trap. "How could I have missed the signs?" Patience thought. Peter was in mortal danger. Greed had spun a web and caught everyone.

The power and influence gained by Greed were immense and had gone unnoticed and undetected. Patience had to return: there was nothing to be done on this side of the planet but everything could be lost forever on the other side, where a young man was heading into disaster and eternal suffering. With every bit of will, Patience headed back to where Peter was being ushered. Aurora raced towards the disturbance on the surface of the water, Peter confident at the tiller. As he approached the vast area of boiling water, Peter was struck by something familiar: the stench of sulphur. He retched at the concentrated vile smell. Suddenly feeling unsure and frightened about where he was heading, Peter attempted to change the direction of his boat, but she would not respond. It seemed that the tiller was set; Peter could not move the tiller. The speed at which he was travelling increased. Sea-spray, salty water, and pungent sulphur made Peter's head spin; he reeled with dizziness and confusion.

Out of control, Aurora headed directly into the boiling water. Peter froze with terror; tears welled and rolled freely down his face. Realisation engulfed him—he was going to die; like his father before him, Peter was going to be lost to the sea! He cried out loud, in the voice of a child, "Mum, help me!"

From hundreds of miles away, Patience watched in horror as the events unfolded around Peter. Focusing all of its will Patience flew towards the stricken boy, travelling at such high speed that the air fractured and split in its path, leaving turbulent contorted air that cracked and thundered. The roar could be heard for tens of miles in all directions. Focussing more intently, Patience hurtled towards the water.

Seen from the ground, it appeared like a comet or shooting star hurtling across the sky, leaving vapour in his wake. Patience dived directly towards the disturbance on the surface of the sea and witnessed the small boat being consumed by the water. There was enough time for a rescue, though. Patience had made it in time, plunging out of the sky, heading with wings folded at its side like a great bird diving to catch its prey. Peter was slumped in the bilges of the boat: one last effort, would do it.

The wind dropped and the acrid sulphur smell overwhelmed his senses. Peter looked at the surface of the sea, millions of tiny bubbles erupting out of the water, all releasing the foul stench. For a moment that seemed to last forever, Aurora came to a full stop, motionless in a sea of bubbles. Everything around Peter suddenly became becalmed, almost silent, and apart from the smell, things seemed to settle. Peter felt a surge of confidence, but this was not to last. The sea and bubbles surrounding him began to collapse. The water had lost its structure. There was no longer buoyancy in the water; the bubbles broke up the water, and the boat started to sink into the dark, repulsive nightmare. The fear that had temporarily lessened being replaced with terror, Peter curled up, holding onto his knees, his head pushed into his arms, he began to sob. When he took a breath, all that he inhaled was thick, stinking sulphur. Peter coughed and retched again. His eyes were stinging; he could not see. His senses were blackening; he was not drowning; he was being suffocated. A body is of no use if it is full of poisonous gases.

Peter fell unconscious. The last thing Peter was aware of was the sound of the loudest crack of thunder he had ever heard; within this sound, he heard the scream, No! Aurora continued to sink through the unholy bubbles. Where there had been water, now there was a void filled with micro-bubbles and darkness—no pressure from the water, just bubbles. The boat sank deeper and deeper, darker and darker into the abyss, out of sight, lost.

With a roar, Patience accelerated towards the sea, then all at once, a terrible noise erupted from the very point of impact as Patience hit an invisible forcefield that reflected his forward motion and repelled it, sending Patience back into the sky. The impact sent out a wave of energy so powerful that the water surrounding the area was vaporised in an instant. Travelling upwards to the sky, the wave of energy hit the clouds, causing them to ignite and explode. The collision sent lightning rods in all directions. Patience had failed.

Chapter 20
Minzo

Travelling at immense speed, the sound struck first, like a heavy hammer blow striking an anvil. The sound amplified a thousand times, cracking eardrums as it passed, then, within seconds, the wave of energy crossed the open sea at a colossal rate, smashing into the small Isle of Minzo, hitting the shore then travelling up the pebbles, colliding with everything in its path. The doors and windows of Peter's home flew wide open; red ridge tiles tore off the roof, glass shattered, the small fire in the hearth was extinguished. Peter's mother, Pearl, screamed in shock at this terrifying event as she ducked and dashed under the kitchen table for cover.

Cries could be heard all around the small community as other homes were engulfed in the powerful wave of energy; also accompanying this wave was the distinctive repulsive smell of decay and sulphur. Smoke billowed from some homes, people ran in all directions, not knowing what to do. Several residents were blown off their feet. As quickly as it had arrived, the wave of destruction vanished from this village, continuing on its destructive journey deeper inland until its energy abated.

Pearl, still in shock, crawled from under the table, retching at the now familiar stench. With terror came another realisation—this was the same smell she thought she had all but forgotten about—the putrid aroma in the air the day her husband David vanished without a trace. Pearl could hear a familiar voice outside. "Pearl, are you ok?" the firm voice of the village elder Bryn called out.

"Pearl, are you hurt?" Bryn called once more; he then saw a movement near the doorway and saw Pearl entering the lightened doorway. She was pale and trembling, her eyes looking past Bryn far out to sea where she could see on the horizon brilliant flashes of lightning. She could hear the booming sounds, and she whispered, "Peter, Peter!" With tears suddenly rushing to her eyes, she then saw Bryn and exclaimed, "My son, Peter!" then she pointed with a shaking finger in the direction of the titanic storm which was raging. Pearl slumped to her knees—she wept.

"Mum, mum!" screamed Joy as she ran along the path to her mother. Joy had been at the school when the wave of energy hit; the school was less effected as it was protected by other buildings. Joy fell to her knees and embraced her mother, holding on so tightly her knuckles were white. Their faces merged, and they both sobbed uncontrollably. They were joined by the elder, Bryn; he bent down and kneeled next to them, talking softly and gently to both Pearl and Joy.

Gathering herself slightly, Pearl took Bryn's hand and allowed him to ease her to her feet. Her eyes stinging with tears and her throat dry, Pearl said in a half-cracking voice, "Peter is out there; how could this happen again?" Fresh tears flowed down her pale cheeks.

Joy, still clinging to her mother, could not speak; she simply looked out across the sea to where the sky was exploding with lightning. Following every metallic crash, a wave of energy travelled across the sea, making landfall within seconds; this continued, almost rhythmically.

With every blast and wave of energy, Pearl winced, and she made such a pained moan that all Bryn could do was to cover her ears in an attempt to lessen her agony. The three of them stood looking out to sea; crowds of villagers joined them, most still in shock, some weeping, some in stunned silence, all looking in the same direction.

Chapter 21
Chaos

L ike magnets thrust together, Patience was repelled from the surface of the sea, the force of opposing wills creating a violent reaction that momentarily weakened both Patience and Greed.

Imprisoned within Greed's will, Chaos sensed that the bondage it was entrapped in faltered every time Patience challenged the will of Greed. Chaos focused and gathered its own will; its power was returning.

Patience gathered its power and again focused, this time looking for any weak spot in the invisible shield which prevented the rescue of Peter, who had now disappeared from sight. Repeatedly crashing into the force field, the sound was carried all around; energy was charging the air, exploding into lightning bolts, but still, the search continued for any weakness.

Chapter 22
Peter

Sinking deeper and deeper into putrid dull green coloured bubbles, Peter's lungs screamed for air, filling instead with thick acrid sulphur, which burned deep into Peter's body. His eyes could not focus; they filled with tears, tears of pain and terror. His mind raced. He thought about his family; then darkness consumed both Peter and his beloved boat Aurora.

With lungs barely able to function, unconsciousness swiftly overwhelmed Peter.

Slumping into the bilges, all senses numbed.

The last thing he heard was the distant sound of pounding, like metal on metal, then nothing. Peter's physical body began to die. The poisonous gases tearing his lungs apart, blood filled the space where tissue once was, his heart faltered as it continued to try in vain to pump lifeblood through Peter's body.

Every missed beat allowed more cells to collapse and perish.

His chest rose and fell fitfully; his body struggled to hold onto life. In the midst of Peter's abject pain and distress, the front of his mind once again summoned powerful images of his family sitting at the dining table. A tangible love surrounded them. The image changed; he was now looking down on the small village where he had grown up, the pebbled beach where he had spent many a happy hour, where he had learned his craft. Peter soared on the thermals, climbing higher in the thin air. All below faded as he ascended, and his remaining senses dulled.

Now there was no more air, no more thoughts as his young ravaged body let go of physical life.

Chapter 23
The Other

Being almost omnipotent, The Other could not see with absolute clarity what the future held in place but was all too aware that the universes must maintain balance; if not, all that existed would be unmade into nothingness, and the universes would be barren. Hints and clues of possibilities were in existence, however, not just for The Other. And that is why The Other had taken great time and care to conceal what was about to awaken within Peters broken body. The seed had travelled undetected within many forms and entities almost since the beginning of time. It was now about to enter into full existence. Balance was in peril. All of the Entities were aware of a convergence. Tension and foreboding gathered momentum.

Chapter 24
The Awakening

B uried deep within this small ravaged shell, the seed that had been planted so long ago suddenly became aware. Its power was immediately vast. Strength silently stealthily started to repair the lifeless body. Peter's essence, his soul, was intact. The Other's attention to the finest of details had been successful. Strength continued to shield its true identity, it appeared as if Peter was still a vulnerable child in a deep sleep, and in Peter's mind, a familiar voice whispered, 'I am with you. You will know what is required when the time is right, for now, go along with matters, 'the voice of Strength then left his mind.

Chapter 25
Greed's Trap

From a distance and barely audible, Peter heard his name being called. Peter felt that he could get closer to this calling and with effort, attempted to call back but to no avail. The hideous darkness once again consumed him, taking all senses and plunging them to nowhere, where nothing existed. Then the voice again, this time louder, closer, "Peter, Peter." In the thick mist shrouding his thoughts, Peter focused; he found strength from within, and he pushed his mind, forcing his mouth to make a sound. With more effort, he willed his eyes to open. All at once, his lungs heaved; he retched as the stinking sulphurous residue within him burst out of every pore in his body. He vomited a greenish-yellow sludge.

His lungs took in a huge breath of air; even though this air was still foul with decay and sulphur, it was more easily accepted into his body. Peter's eyes began to focus.

His body began to feel. He was lying on a cold hard surface; the light his eyes could see was not light but smoky green dimness.

Through this dimness, Peter slowly focused his eyes; he saw the outline of a person standing above him. 'Careful, careful,' his inner voice urged. "Peter, that is it, you are safe." Moving his body which felt heavy and cumbersome, Peter lifted his head.

His chest ached, and his stomach was sore, but he continued to lift himself; a hand grabbed his hand, and a strong jerking pull got Peter into a sitting position. Peter's eyes continued to focus on his surroundings;

he was now sitting in the centre of what seemed like a cave, but more than a cave as it had some sort of rough-looking furniture. He concluded that this was not a cave but rather the inside of a tumbled, run-down building. The person standing next to him was still out of focus because of the poor light; then, the person spoke again. "Peter, you are safe now; nothing can harm you here. Oh, Peter, I thought I would never see you again."

At this last statement, Peter's focus sharpened considerably; his mind heard the words but could not make sense of them, then quite suddenly, realisation crashed into his thoughts. "I know the voice. I recognise the silhouette standing in front of me. This can not be happening," he thought. "Father, father, is that you?" Peter exclaimed.

There was a brief silence, then came the answer that Peter could not believe; his mind raced, his heart pounded, he felt warm tears erupting in his eyes. "Yes, it is me, Peter."

More tears flowed down the young man's face, like electricity surging through his very soul. Still, more tears came.

Even as the weight of the last few seconds sunk into Peter's mind, the room he was in seemed to alter; shimmering, familiar shapes came into focus. "Is it possible that we are in our own home?" the question seemed to slam into Peter's mind. This had been a dream; it must have been, all of it: the water, the voices, the bubbles, all a strange, almost real dream. And now he was waking up, and all was well; his father was there with his mother and Joy. This was unbelievable. All around the space unseen by Peter was movement, black putrid slime undulating, pulsing, dark spark like eruptions created a fizzing electric environment. The space was alive with lost, trapped souls, more dark sparks emanated from the entombed, it seemed that there was an unholy excitement in this place. The lair was charged with vile evil intent. "Where is mum?" The question came so innocently, so naively, so childlike, almost choked out on a tiny voice. "We are alone, Peter; your mother is not here. We are in a better place, a place where we can be together. No more fishing, no more hard work—just us, forever." Like a bolt through his heart, Peter exclaimed, "But we love to fish. I love mum and want us all to be together. I don't want us to be separated. I want us all as one." The words came out in a harsh tone. This even surprised Peter. "That is not important, boy. It is us now. Get used to it!" These words were spoken in an almost sneering, rasping tone, a dangerous tone. Peter looked up in surprise into his father's face.

Peter said nothing. A weak smile broke across his father's face, then he turned around and left the room. "We will talk later; rest, and I will send you food. Eat; you will need your strength." Something troubled Greed as he left the room, something that he knew so well, yet could not explain, yet familiar. Alertness was required. The more energy Greed used to back up this trap, the more Chaos sensed the situation and waited.

Peter, with little effort, stood and went to a small wooden cot bed where he sat a while wondering about what had just taken place, his father, and what was going to happen to him. A wave of tiredness swept over Peter, and he quickly fell into a deep sleep. While he slept, somewhere in his mind, he could still hear the constant sound of metal on metal, almost rhythmical, not loud but there in his mind; in some way, he felt slightly comforted by the sound. Then as soft as the fluttering wings of a butterfly, Peter heard a familiar voice in his head, a whisper so quiet it was almost silent: "I am with you." Peter's mind replied so positively and equally as silently,

"I know." His inner-self rested and became at peace. Peter was now aware of Strength.

He always knew he had it within him but had not even thought about it, but now Strength had ignited in the innermost parts of Peters mind. He realised that he must keep this hidden from all.

Chapter 26
Anger

Time was of no concern where Peter now found himself, so when Peter woke up again, he had no idea how long he had slept. He did not know if it was day or night as the same dull green, yellow light had not changed. He was aware, however, that he was not alone. "Father, is that you?" Peter asked in a quiet voice. "Yes, boy, there is food for you; come and eat." this was not a request. This was more of an order. "Yes, father," Peter said, rising from the cot. Peter noticed the air was still heavy with the sultry smell of damp decay and sulphur, but he had no trouble breathing; in fact, he felt no fatigue at all. His chest had no discomfort, and his eyes were no longer sore; he could see rather well. He glanced around the room, looking more closely at the details in this space. It could have been his home. Peter sat at the table. On a platter of what looked like driftwood sat a fish; he had not seen this sort before. It had angry teeth and wide red eyes and appeared to still have slime on its skin.

The fish twitched. "Eat boy, eat," the words came from a tight mouth. "But it doesn't look cooked, father." "That is how we like it here. Eat it." There was tension in the air. Peter could detect this but did not say anything. He picked up the fish and bit into the slimy flesh, which was not too difficult; the taste, however, was dreadful, even rancid. He ate all the same, excusing himself halfway through the terrible food. Strength told him that he would not suffer from eating this fish, that he should not react in any way. Too late, Peter threw up, the fish landed at his feet, steam rose from the flesh, and it twitched. Nothing was said. Peter sat upright and said, "Father, we thought you were dead, that we would never see you again. What happened to you? How did you get here?" "Questions, questions. I got here the same way you did—I saw the water looking like it had fish, so I sailed to it, then I realised that the surface was not really water, but bubbles and I sank. I was saved and brought here, and here is where I have been ever since. Happy now?"

"But you have not aged. You look the same, father. What have you been doing all of this time? Why didn't you try to come home?" "Questions, questions, you ask too many questions. Time means nothing here, so I have not aged, and I could not get out, so I stayed. Does that finally answer your questions, questions, questions?" The reply was in the same harsh tones as the previous conversation, but there was more; Peter could sense impatience, he detected anger. Peter said, "Father, you have changed. I love you, so why are you so angry with me?" With an eruption of anger, Peter's father pushed the table away and stood. His body seemed to grow for an instant then revert again, Peter's father turned and walked out of the room, leaving Peter in silence.

Deep in Peter's mind and out of detection, he heard the word "Caution!" Greed immediately flinched and cast a concerned glance before leaving.

Chapter 27
Patience

At the same moment that Peter's father seemed to lose his temper knocking the table out of the way, high above them, Patience sensed a loss of will and focus and felt a weakness in the invisible shield below. Patience now focused and located what he was looking for.

With a more determined force of will, Patience pounded one area, further weakening the energy field; thunderous crashes and lightning intensified. Chaos readied itself.

Pearl, Joy and Bryn, along with the rest of the community, took cover on the shore as the energy waves came faster and more furious, smashing into Minzo.

In abject terror, Pearl and the others simply huddled together. No one uttered a word; they simply froze almost to the spot, minds frozen, unable to deal with what was taking place in front of them.

Chapter 28
David

Peter knew that he was in great danger. He felt that something was terribly wrong with his father. It must be the influence of the place on him. He knew that he must find him and try to talk him into returning home from wherever they were.

It was better than doing nothing at all, he said to himself. Getting to his feet, Peter looked for the doorway; strangely, he had not thought about how his father came and went. Peter looked to where the door was in his own home, and he saw what looked like a door, but not quite a door. In fact, the closer he looked at the room, the more it appeared to alter, not the room in his house but reverting to the dark, damp space surrounded by decay. His mind told Peter that the danger was more intense. Peter approached the space where the door should have been. It was almost transparent; he could see through the facade into a vast dimness. Peter said to himself, "I must be silent and out of sight." As if the thought was an instruction, Peter felt himself alter slightly but did not know in what way. His senses felt so alert, so focused. He felt calm. He was more aware of his surroundings, and when he turned around to see where he was in relation to the table he had been sitting at, he saw only space and the shimmering outline of the table vanishing before his eyes. Now there was nothing.

He was standing in a space without any limits; no walls, no ceilings, no real light, a void. He stood for a while, wondering which direction he should go to look for his father. He then saw a shape in the distance; it looked like a man. The person was standing over a large box or table of some kind. Peter thought, "Could this be father?" He was about to call, but before he could form the words in his mind, he heard a sharp "No," and the compulsion to shout to his father vanished. Peter thought about this and realised that his inner-strength had taken over for that brief moment. "But why, it is only my father," he thought. Peter walked slowly and quietly towards his father. The figure was getting larger, and Peter could see more details. His father was bending over what appeared to be a large square rock. He appeared to be pushing his hands onto something which was on top of the slab of rock. Peter closed in, he saw more detail, then he inhaled a sharp intake of stale air—his father's hands seemed to enter the thing on the slab, a body who Peter recognised was his father. Whoever it was that he had thought was his father had his hands deep inside the chest cavity. Several fingerlike tendrils were penetrating the victim's temples. His father on the slab moaned pathetically. The thing whose hands were inside his chest muttered to himself. Peter gingerly moved even closer and heard the muttering of this monster: "More Soul, how much more Soul to convince the brat?" The words were belched out; they came out like a fire crackling on dried-out grass.

Peter took in another involuntary gasp of foul air. This time the figure stopped and turned around, looking directly at where Peter stood. Peter held his breath and stood still. Standing in front of him, looking at him, was something that had the appearance of his father but was not his father. Peter looked more intently at this 'father' look alike; he saw that the flesh was almost transparent. Under the skin, there appeared to be movement. He could not see beyond this. It was the face that shocked Peter; where there was a face, now there was a boiling mass of sultry green and yellow quarter light. It resembled a mass of eels trapped in a dried-out waterhole.

Set deep where the eyes were, Peter saw two deeper vile-looking spots of moving light; when these lights turned to face Peter, they brightened, flashing red with hatred. The eyes, however did not focus on Peter—they seemed to look through Peter into him. They also looked puzzled. The thing withdrew its arms from within the body on the slab. Peter's true father groaned again. "Where are you? Do you think you can hide from meeee?" The voice was not a voice as we know but a terrifying noise put together to form words. There was great anger and danger in the noise; as the words were spoken, the air around Peter cracked and stabbed at his skin. The air tore away at Peter's clothing; putrid air assaulted his nostrils. Peter could feel weight on him; it felt like he was being crushed. Fear began to rise in his heart—beads of sweat bubbles on his forehead.

"You are mine. You have always been mine from the very beginning, but only now can I take you, now that I have you here in this place. Your physical being is of no importance to me. It is what lies within you. Oh yes, you thought I could not see you. I have always known you were there and now you will join with me. I will gain the upper hand, and you will look up to meeee, you will obey meee. You will be my tool to do with as I see fit." Peter could feel his skin burning. The thing in front of him could see him clearly.

The thing stepped closer to Peter. There was now no real person standing in front of him; instead, in its place was a writhing mass of slithering movement being contained within some sort of clear gelatinous covering. A force of pure evil energy emanated from this creature, and it moved closer to Peter.

On the slab, Peter saw the emaciated, weak body of his father. The body was clothed in rags. Barely audible noises came from his mouth, then Peter saw his father's eyes slowly begin to open. His head turned, and Peter saw that his father's head was facing towards him, and a tear fell from his father's eye. His eyes, however shocked Peter, for they were white milky orbs, unseeing, filled with pain and unimaginable suffering. Peter was able to make out the words that slowly came to his father's lips: "I love you Pe... ," then nothing as the sentence was not completed. The body on the slab stiffened and became still, the fraction of colour that remained in his face vanished. Inside Peter's mind, he sensed that although it appeared that his father had died, somehow Peter was sure that he was still alive, just. Peter rushed to be at his father's side, trying to avoid the monster in front of him. He dodged, but as he approached his father's resting place, Peter was swept backwards off his feet by a massive jolt of energy, so powerful that it sent him flying through the dimness, landing heavily on his back. Peter caught his breath and again ran forward, realising that the impact had no real effect on his body. Once again, as he attempted to get to his father, the monster was able to bar his route; another burst of pure will connected with Peter, instantly sending him in another direction.

This time Peter was aware that his assailant had somehow flown in the opposite direction to that of Peter. The monster lay silent on the ground for a moment then roared, 'You dare to smite me, me!' the noise was deafening, sparks of fiery red evil hatred flashed in every direction, the black slime surrounding the place convulsed in shock.

Peter got to his feet and walked slowly towards his dying father and once again in his path was the creature. Peter detected a difference in the way the creature stalked him. "He is being cautious," Peter thought, then without warning, the attack took place. Taking the form of Peter's father again, the monster approached Peter. "He is mine. You will never have him," the monster hissed the words, "You will bend at my knee forever. I have you. You, too, are mine. It has always been so, for I am the strongest, the chosen." The words were spoken with such anger and hatred; like in a tantrum the monster hurled threats at Peter. He stood his ground as the assault was launched. The monster struck Peter with every bit of hatred it had. The collision between both created such a thundering noise that Peter felt he was inside an explosion, but very little happened to him; he could feel that he was surrounded by a field of light that absorbed the impact. He wondered why he felt so calm in the face of such horror. He then realised that rather than him being sent flying across the void, it was the monster who was sent careering out of control, landing some distance away.

Dazed and disoriented, the monster again lay on its back on the damp rancid ground, not able to comprehend what had just taken place. A rage so intense began to build within the monster, but for this moment, it was incapable of responding; frozen, it lay there. Peter went to his father; he took his father's hand in his and said in a soft tone, "Father, I am here, you are safe, I will take care of you." There was no movement from his father, and Peter knew that his father was dying. Peter held him tightly. He could sense his father's energy leaving the frail body. The white light that enrobed Peter then began to close around the dying body of David. The light seemed to gently massage the frail body. David made a quiet, comforting sound.

Chapter 29
The Rescue

High above the turbulent water, Patience continued the search for the weakness in the barrier. The sense of urgency grew within him, then all of a sudden, Patience felt that the 'will' keeping the barrier stable begin to falter, briefly at first, then again for a second time. On the third occasion, Patience found the chink in the armour that he was searching for.

Gathering great will Patience plunged through the tear in the energy field, diving like a fire-bolt deeper through the decaying micro-bubbles, deeper into the dark, putrid green-yellow environment, then bursting into the void where Peter and his father were together. Taking in the details of the circumstances at once, Patience landed in human form next to Peter. He looked at Peter and his father and, with a raised eyebrow, acknowledged the white light that surrounded both men. Patience had taken the form of an athlete, and he towered over Peter and said, "We are in danger. My Brother will gather his will any time now and attack again. I fear that his rage and hatred will not be contained. We must leave this vile place at once."

Patience took Peter by the arm and then gently picked the dying body of David up. He looked up to where he had entered this decaying space and said, "It is time."

Chapter 30
Tears

O n the shoreline, taking cover from the repeating crashes of thunder and lightning and wave after wave of energy, Pearl and Joy together with the rest of the community stared into the distance as the intensity of the noise and lightning grew. Then with the loudest booming crash, the continuing metal-on-metal sound abruptly stopped; the last wave of energy came and went. There seemed to be a stillness and quietness that lasted forever. Pearl thought to herself, "Is this the quiet before the main storm?" As she looked on into the distance, she saw one shaft of blue-white light shoot out of the water and vanish into the sky. She also knew that nothing could have survived the madness of what had taken place, and Pearl quietly wept.

Chapter 31
Self Sacrifice

P atience was about to leave with both Peter and David when Peter removed his huge hand holding him and said, "You will take my father to my safe place where he can be healed. I must stay." Peter looked into the deep brown eyes of Patience and in that moment passed on the location of his 'safe place'

The safe place he had remembered was for the occasion when he was in great need; now was that time, as the great need was to save the life of his father. He then said, "You will not return to this place. You will return David to his home; he has endured enough." Patience was taken aback by this command; even though it was given in a kind tone, nevertheless, it was a command.

Patience knew what was needed to be done, and without argument, he cradled David into his arms. The intensity of light surrounding David grew stronger, and in a shaft of blue-white light, they vanished above into the darkness. Getting back to his feet, Greed gathered itself and stealthily moved forward. Peter was so aware and prepared himself, standing firm and watching as Greed approached. Then as Greed got closer, his mass began to increase. The feeling of pressure in the void multiplied; a madness entered the void. Peter could feel the anger emanating from Greed—building and building. Greed grew to a towering height. The transparent outer covering containing him shimmered, within him a writhing mass of movement, coming and going out of focus.

The entire space was charged with energy. Greed stopped ahead of Peter and, in a voice that cracked the air, stated, "You are going to be my plaything, I will own you, and whatever dwells within you will be mine forever, forever." His anger was turning to madness. Where there should have been eyes, instead there were blazing holes of angry red fire, spitting out flames. In an instant, Greed in his giant form reached down and grabbed hold of Peter. Huge claw-like hands engulfed him. The sound of sizzling began as Greed screamed in an increasingly distorted voice, "There is no escape, I now own you, you are mine, you are..."

The words stopped abruptly, what was a distorted face began to contort even further; the eye sockets widened as Greed dropped Peter to the ground. The light surrounding Peter began to grow brighter and brighter. The dim light in the void was illuminated with pure white light. The void had no limits; it was simply space. The light emanating from Peter continued to brighten. Greed lifted his huge distorted limbs and shielded his red hot eye sockets, then exploding into incandescent light. Peter said, "No! You will never take me just because you want to. I am not yours, I am myself, and you cannot have me." The words slammed into Greed; he staggered backwards, the giant form began to shrink, and he screamed in a sort of mad agony. The boiling mass under the transparent skin darkened, splits began to open up, revealing steaming blackened entrails which fell out of him spilling onto the damp floor; the entrails steamed and hissed as they landed. Greed continued to scream in a hideous snarling voice, reducing in size then shifting his appearance to human form. Then silence. The incandescent light that surrounded Peter lessened, and Peter stood in front of what appeared to be the form of his father David again. The light reduced to a soft glow, and Peter said, "The time has come for you to stop what you are doing. You have created hurt amongst the human race. You have encouraged hatred and greed. The human race was never yours to do your bidding; this planet is the rarest of them all, it must not be spoilt simply because you want it for yourself. This planet and the human race will be allowed to evolve without your evil influence. There must again be balance, no longer individuals who use their energy to create wrong and hurt. Neither will you ever take me as your own ; you cannot have me. I have never been yours for the taking. Instead and to give this planet the peace and time it needs to repair from your will and to survive, I will give myself to you, freely. I will walk with you. I will guide you. I will free you from your misguided route, I will be your brother."

Chapter 32
Greed

Greed stood trembling, eruptions of foul green energy smashed all around the blackness, agitated, cracking and fracturing the space they were in. All of the energy was focusing from where Greed stood motionless. In the darkness a vortex appeared, swirling with flashing lightning; it roared with contorted screams.

The whole of the space charged with evil will. The pressure within the space built, and Peter felt himself becoming overwhelmed. His inner-light was not able to repel the intensity of evil will. Peter fell backwards. Still, Greed gathered more dreadful will, the vortex flashed, then there was silence. The space filled with the odour of death, as the souls of millions of murdered entities, entered the space willing to do their master's bidding.

Greed trembled with a rage that was felt throughout all of the universes. In a terrible roar, the words *'NEVER'* erupted from within the creature. The words slammed into Peter further pinning him to the ground; his light flickered and faded, his protection waned under the almighty will of Greed, and then his light was extinguished.

Greed again roared as his crushing weight of evil enveloped Peter. Peter watched from within the tangible hatred; he saw Greed trembling with unholy rage and desire, he felt Greed's exultation and triumph, he waited for the inevitable to take its course.

However, a pure calmness entered Peter; he was now prepared for his fate. Peter knew this moment, he accepted it. After all it was one of the possibilities.

Greed gathered it's insane will, preparing to release it and destroy Peter, after of course Peter's power had been consumed and absorbed. Greed screamed at Peter in a million terrible voices, 'I take, I am not given, I take. You, you think you can give to me, you think you can guide me, I take, you do not give, *I take, I take, I take!*'

Greed unleashed its entire will at Peter. Peter immediately felt the excruciating pain of evil pounding at him, overwhelming him, tearing at his soul. Greed's features no longer resembled anything. It was pure energy; a hatred never witnessed before enveloped Peter. The energy force driven at Peter completely consumed him. As he was slipping out of existence, Peter was aware of another entity. While Greed concentrated all of its might and energy on Peter, it released its grasp and control over Chaos.

Released from its incarceration Chaos received a renewed will, a will that shielded Peter's soul before it was destroyed by Greed.

Peter vanished, leaving Greed alone in the void. Stillness and silence followed Peter's exit. Greed was quite alone, its will then turned on itself. Slowly the particles that were Greed began to twitch. They became agitated. The agitation grew and grew. Like a supernova, Greed grew and grew; dark energy surrounded its whole existence, then the mass started to collapse in on itself. Dreadful cracking noises, terrible screams emanated.

In a sound that was heard everywhere, Greed's final word was *'NEVER!* At that moment every atom, every detail, every part of its will imploded then instantaneously starburst outwards. In that moment the essence of Greed was scattered throughout the universes and a shock wave followed and for a microsecond, all light in existence flickered. Greed was no more. In another part of the universes—The Other was saddened.

Chapter 33
The Safe Place

Peter stood in the 'safe place'. He wondered about what had taken place; it seemed such a short window of time. He held no frightened thoughts. He had no anger or malice.

He simply knew that matters had taken place and that he was part of it, almost as an observer. "It is done, my son," the voice of The Other spoke.

Peter said, "What has become of Greed?" The 'safe place' began to shimmer, and where there had been nothing, now there was a table and chairs. On the table were five crystal glasses containing pure water. Sitting at the end of the table was a woman; she had iridescent blue-white hair, her eyes were violet, and she glowed. She smiled a warm smile. "Take a seat, Peter," she said in kind tones. Peter sat down, and instinctively he picked up the glass in front of him and took a long deep drink of the pure water. Peter could feel the water entering him; he felt that his whole being was being cleansed. He realised that he knew this place and also that he knew the woman who sat in front of him. He said, "I am home." The woman replied, "Yes, you are, and your name is Compassion and Love."

Chapter 34
The Homecoming

On the pebble shoreline of the Isle of Minzo, the gathered village community stood in sullen silence. The smashing sounds and waves of energy were gone, the sea was again calm, and the sky was soft blue. Pearl stood holding the hand of her daughter Joy. No words were spoken, but love flowed between them, the love of a mother for her children. The tears had all but dried up, and Bryn said, "We must return to our homes. Much has taken place on this day. We must repair our buildings and carry on living."

It seemed that the whole community heard these words and turned to face the land, then a voice from the crowd called, "Look, a man over there!" In the distance, a man slowly moved towards them. Pearl looked more closely, and with a rush of emotion, called out, "Peter, Peter, you are safe!" Pearl ran, still holding tight onto Joy's hand. Bryn behind her, Pearl ran with her heart pounding in her chest. "Peter! Peter!" Pearl called. Then Pearl stopped in her tracks as though she had hit some invisible wall; her eyes widened, tears welled up, and ran down her soft features. Standing on the pebbles in front of Pearl and Joy was not Peter but David, Pearl's lost husband. David had not altered since the day he went missing; he was even wearing the same clothes, only they appeared to be brand new. The only difference was David's eyes; where before he had beautiful brown eyes, in their place now were white orbs, unseeing, stolen.

Behind Pearl, Bryn fell to his knees and, looking to the skies, began to speak softly. Pearl, realising that David could not see her, slowly moved toward her husband.

When she got in front of him, she took his hand and placed it on her cheek. The white orbs filled with tears and fell down David's face. He reached forward and embraced his wife, then Joy put her arms around her father's middle and held him firmly. "Father, oh, father," was all she could say. The powerful emotions lasted for several minutes. The gathered crowd spoke softly to one another; shock, wonder, and bewilderment spread, but more than that, thanks filled the air.

David took Pearl's hands and placed them on either side of his face, then he removed them and said, "Peter, it was Peter, he saved me." "What do you mean, David?" Pearl said gently. David said, "All I remember is that I sort of woke up, and Peter spoke to me, and he told his friend to take me and look after me, then I was on this beach, and I heard you calling. Peter saved me." Pearl said softly, "Let us go home; we can talk there."

Tears again began to drop from her eyes as they walked slowly back to their home.

Chapter 35
The Gathering

Peter knew that what the woman said was true: he had always known who he was. With a shimmer of light, a tall, athletic man appeared and took his place at the table. The woman said, "Patience, welcome." In a gesture of utmost respect, Patience bowed his head—no words needed to be spoken.

Very soon after the arrival of Patience another person arrived shimmering out of blue-white light. It was an older thin man with grey hair. He too was surrounded by light. The woman said, "Welcome, Chaos," again with an acknowledgement of deepest respect Chaos bowed his head.

Both then lifted up the glass in front of them and drank deeply before placing the glass back on the table. Peter said, pointing to the fifth crystal glass, "And who is this glass for?" Looking saddened and with a tear in her eyes, the woman said, "This is for Greed." "Greed?" Peter said. "Yes, for Greed, as it is my wish that in some other time, Greed will once again sit at my table as he had done before he erred." Peter said, "What happened to Greed?" The woman replied, "You had a choice, as did Greed. You chose to give your existence to save mankind. This choice could only be made by you. You could have chosen to destroy Greed as you possess the will, but you chose to show pity and compassion. You are love, and this is what you wanted to give to your brother. Greed had forgotten about love and compassion too long ago; he craved power, domination, and hatred. Your act of compassion was so shocking to Greed that his very existence could not accept the gift.

In his rage, he simply threw himself into the universes, scattered like dust on the wind. Chaos had to make a choice at the same time, choosing to offer you protection from Greed's fury, for, at that time, your resistance was very weak as your offer to stay with Greed was genuine; you opened your heart to Greed and Chaos shielded you and assisted your exit to your 'safe place'. Chaos made a choice. That choice freed him from the will of Greed." Peter asked, 'but was Greed unmade?' The Other replied, 'My dear son, you have a lot to learn, and in time you will know that which is intended for you to know. It is forbidden to unmake anything, Greed was scattered through time and space, but still remains.' The woman sighed and said, "Our tasks are many, and from this time forward, your tasks are to deliver the human race from the peril started by Greed. This planet is unique. It has to be cared for throughout the rest of time." The woman then said to Peter, "My Son, you will take your place again at my side and with your brothers will bring once again balance to be." Then as an afterthought, she said, "Peter, visit your earthly mother and quiet her grief." With this comment, the table was gone, as were the others. Peter stood knowing his task and set to it.

Following the return of David, lots of questions were asked, but David was unable to answer them. He had no knowledge of the circumstances of disappearance or of how long he had been lost; the only memory he kept was his blurred recollection of Peter. Pearl's grief stayed in the front of her mind constantly, although she was so happy that David was now returned and safe, losing her son could not be reconciled. The love Pearl held in her heart for her son, her firstborn, was profound, a sadness so heavy Pearl could barely contain it; indeed she went for long walks, and when she thought she was out of sight, she would crumble with the weight of grief, sobbing until no more tears would leave her eyes. Pearl was, however, not alone. Her link to Peter was strong.

After supper consisting of fresh cornbread and fish, Pearl went to her bed; she eventually fell to sleep. Pearl was then aware of light, dim at first but getting lighter. She was scared and attempted to shield her eyes. "Is this another nightmare?" she said to herself. "Mother, I am with you. I am at your side." Letting her hands drop, Pearl looked around. She could see the outline of her son Peter. Her heart pounded; the love she had inside almost burst with joy. It was a mother's love. Pearl reached out and touched Peter on his face. Her hand stayed there, touching his face. Within that touch, Pearl knew the destiny of her son. She also knew the love he had for her and his earthly family, and she smiled. Pearl realised that she had always known about her son, but when giving it thought, the idea simply went out of reach, and she thought about something else. Pearl reached up and kissed Peter on the forehead. He seemed to have grown. Peter said, "I am forever with you, mother. Think of this place as your safe place. Whenever you are in need, think of being here, and you will be. I will always be here waiting. I love you, mother, now and forever." The sleep that Pearl sank into was deep and restful.

The following morning, when David and Joy went into the kitchen, the feeling of emotional weight was no longer present. Without a word, David found his chair, which was next to Joy. Joy took her father's hand and gently squeezed it. There was no need for words as they could hear Pearl. She was standing in front of the stove, slowly turning the creamy porridge, humming her favourite tune. She was happy and content—grief was nowhere to be found.

Chapter 36
Greed

Deep in the core of the planet Earth, squeezed into the tightest of fissures, fragments of something moved. Looking more closely at what was there, it resembled a writhing mass of eels trapped in a dried-out pond. The smell of sulphur was intense. Tiny micro-bubbles oozed from the scene. There was a noise emanating from this unholy mass; it seemed to say very clearly, "Never!"

THE PRESSURE

Chapter 1
The Attack

As the pressure started to build, his head ached. Trying to find a comfortable position in which to sit, Ash fidgeted. "My head, what's going on?"

Ash felt his teeth begin to hurt; his gums started to bleed, still the pressure continued to build. He stood up from his computer desk and placed his hands palms down. Ash shook his head then he caught a glimpse of himself in the wall mirror to his side and with a sharp intake of breath, his whole body froze, his eyes widened, and his blood ran cold within his veins. In the reflection, Ash could see himself, pale-faced, his focus shifting in and out, but what had caused this reaction, he could barely believe he could see: surrounding his whole body was an iridescence that moved in and out of focus. The colour was grey-black but when it came into focus Ash could see surrounding him was a demon. The grotesque claws of the demon were around his head, pushing both sides in, the black tendril-like fingers penetrating his skull trying to reach his brain, attempting to locate his soul. Ash knew it was a demon, but he also recognised certain features; a brief feeling of pity came over Ash.

Without thinking, Ash visualised a protective shield within him, starting at his core and emanating outwards, making certain that his thoughts were tightly controlled and hidden from this demon. The shield coursed through his veins and reached just under his skin, waiting undetected, gathering strength and focus.

Looking more closely around the room, he noticed

that there was a sort of dark red-brown, almost black-coloured blood-slime dripping from small cracks in the walls, pulsating as it slowly flowed; he also saw black blowflies massing in front of the windows. The erratic buzzing sound grew louder until it was one gross nauseating drone. "How, why?" Ash asked himself.

Ash had the vision firmly constructed in his mind. He released the image using his will to direct a powerful shield to travel from within himself. The force of his will created a near-explosion of energy that contacted the demon head-on, repelling the creature in an instant. The demon screamed a chilling hateful noise and smashed into the wall seeming to stick to where the slime was oozing. The demon was stuck to the wall, and the slime began to cover its dreadful body. It made inhuman noises and cursed Ash, 'This is not over!' It spat the words out then again screamed as it was consumed by the slime, all disappearing at once, leaving no trace of the evil creature.

Ash sat down heavily on the bed. The effort required to focus his will had weakened him; however, he remained alert and on guard as he also knew that he was vulnerable to another attack at any time. Wondering why he had not been aware of this assault concerned Ash. "Why didn't I sense him? How could I have let this happen?" he said to himself. *'More practice, I must focus and practice, I can not allow this to happen again!'* Now deep in thought, he concentrated and recalled the first encounter.

Chapter 2
The Family

Twelve months earlier, Ash went to help an old university pal, Brian. Brian and Ash had been friends for many years but had lost contact when Ash relocated to the Scottish Highlands, where the lifestyle, environment, and job suited him.

Brian contacted Ash; he had a problem.

"I can't talk about it over the phone. Can you please come down? I need to talk to you, I know we haven't spoken for a while, but I have done something terrible and do not know what to do."

"What is it? What can I do?" Ash asked, slightly taken aback by the directness from Brian.

"Please, I just need your help! Sensing that Brian genuinely needed help and because Ash simply had it in him to help others, "I will come as soon as," Ash said. In fact, he felt so much urgency in Brian's tone, he packed his car and was on the road within the hour. 'What has Brian been up to? What could be so terrible?' Ash thought to himself as he collected a few items ready to leave.

Travelling through the Highlands, Ash realised that his choice to relocate had been the right one. Driving along, he had some of the most outstanding scenery anywhere on the planet: magnificent mountains, huge skies, uninterrupted views at almost every turn, and of course, the fresh, clean air. Ash stopped his car on top of Rannoch Moor simply to take in the scene; he had done this so many times, but the view always held something very special for him. Taking in several deep breaths of air, he felt himself completely relaxing.

While standing in the light breeze looking in the direction of Bridge of Orchy, he was aware of a voice. He looked around but could not see anything until he looked back to where he had begun looking, and standing a couple of paces away was a woman. She was probably in her forties, maybe a lot older; he could not tell. She was about five feet tall with long silver or was it grey hair? The hair seemed to catch the light of the sun, or was it an illusion? as her hair seemed to shimmer. Her clothes were simple, appearing like soft cotton, pale blue.

Her eyes were hazel brown and sparkled as bright as a star. The woman smiled at Ash, without any thought, he smiled back and said, "You made me jump, I didn't see you coming."

The woman stepped closer to Ash, she smiled a smile that seemed to put Ash at even more ease, and then she said, "Ash, you must be careful. Where you go, there is great danger, and you will need protection!"

"How do you know what my name is?" Ash asked, a little surprised. The woman said, "That is not important, what is I must now share with you. My time here is limited. You must listen and take clear note of what I tell you."

"Of course I will." Ash answered as a pupil to the teacher but not knowing why he was obeying someone who he had just this very second met. There was something about this woman. His thought was abruptly halted when the woman said, "I have only a limited time, so you must take note and practice." Then she said, "I want you to think about the person who means the most to you, now think about the love you have for that person." Ash thought about his mother. He was extremely close to his mother; even though they lived some distance apart, he spoke and made contact with her daily.

"Yes, I sense it, good, now focus on that feeling." Ash strained to locate what he was feeling.

"No, you are not focusing, you are trying too hard. You must let the sense of love build within you. You must see it within you."

Ash began to tremble with the exertion and concentration.

"That is much better; you are doing well. You know you have the ability to protect yourself; you simply need to focus and use it, now expand it through your whole body."

"What do you mean?" Ash said.

"Ash, you must see within yourself, as if your feeling of love is like a balloon. You must expand the balloon, let it grow, send it outwards until you have surrounded yourself in the pure love you feel, like a bubble and hold it."

Ash concentrated and all at once he appeared to be surrounded by a film of shimmering energy, even light.

"Yes! Ash, you have done it. I knew you would." Ash was slightly bemused about this whole encounter. He said, "Who are you and why have you instructed me in this way, what do you know?" The woman looked into his eyes. In that look, something struck Ash; somehow, he knew this woman.

"Yes, and about time," she said, slightly amused. "And yes, I am your grandmother," she said with a warm, loving smile.

Ash said, "But I didn't know you. You died before I was one-year-old."

She replied in such a gentle tone, "Ash, my dear boy, when you were born, your mother handed you into my arms; at that moment we were bonded more closely than you can ever know. At that moment, I spoke with you, and you reassured me that you had the gift; how else could you have spoken to me?" Ash said, "But I don't understand; how could I have spoken to you, and why don't I remember anything, even you?"

"Ash, my dearest boy, to have known what you possess at such an early time in your development could have ruined your life. Just as you, others in your family have a special gift: some are aware, some are not."

Ash said, "But why now, what has changed? Why have you come now?"

"I have not just come. I have never left your side. But now you must learn how to use what is yours; you are in danger, from what that is not clear. My time is so limited in this form, Ash. Know that I am and will always be with you. Practice, practice, and know what is within you. I love you my dear, dear boy." The woman disappeared, her image blending into the breathtaking scenery.

Standing quite still in the silence, his attention was abruptly shattered by the blast of car horn, then a loud foreign voice shouted. "Gee is this the Highland?" the American tourist asked Ash.

"Yeah, that's right, the Highland it is!" Ash turned around and went back to his waiting car. Getting in, he continued his journey, his mind in overdrive.

Chapter 3
Friendship

Ash met Brian while they were training at University; both had chosen to be lawyers and their friendship strengthened and grew. They shared a flat; they shared knowledge, testing each other on their individual subjects. You might say that they both learned two arms of the law. They enjoyed the fact that they were able to help one another. Brian was studying business law, while Ash studied family law. Both men were smart; Ash was a more caring person, while Brian had a hunger to achieve highly within his chosen subject.

The years passed and both men graduated. Ash began work for a local solicitors' group; they specialised in divorce issues. Brian began work at a high-profile business partnership in the centre of Manchester. Both Ash and Brian remained close friends; however, their workloads meant that getting together for a pint became a rarer event. They did call each other and chat about current work issues. It seemed that Brian was indeed striving to get a name for himself as he had already climbed a couple of rungs of the partnership ladder. Ash, on the other hand became almost bogged down with the highly emotional issues which needed to be presented in a divorce court.

While Brian devoured case after case and continued to climb the ladder, Ash became more concerned about what was happening to children who found themselves in the centre of an unholy row between their parents. He could see the hurt that was being inflicted onto the children. Most of the time, the selfish parents were blind to the needs of their children, which was probably why they were not capable of maintaining a happy family life—they were emotionally blind.

Soon Ash needed to move on—he had applied to the social services in the Highlands. Ash was well overqualified for the position offered, but he felt he could help kids who needed help, and so with a sense of relief, he upped his roots and moved the 400 miles into the Highlands, to a small village not too far from Fort William. Ash settled into a small one-bed croft. The croft was surrounded by outstanding mountain and sea scenery; almost immediately, Ash felt that he was 'home'. He settled into his new job, and even though his salary was much less, Ash had not been so happy in years.

On hearing the news that Ash had actually made that stupid move to the arse end of nowhere, Brian almost spat, "Stupid bastard! Why there, why so far away, what about me?"

Chapter 4
Mark Trenter

Ambition is all well and good, providing you stay in control of it and don't let ambition control you.

Brian was very good at his job. His rapid ascent within the partnership turned heads; he was a 'flier', and he would stamp on anyone in his path. The CEO recognised this; he also saw in Brian, a trait that he too was only too aware of—Brian's hunger to get to the top as quickly as possible. The CEO kept a close eye on Brian.

Sitting at his large rosewood desk in a massive wood-paneled room was the CEO of Brian's firm of lawyers, Mark Trenter. He was fifty-four years of age and had a wife and three children; they lived in a large house on the outskirts of Manchester. Mr Trenter had an apartment within the company building. Waiting for him there was a woman who he had been having an affair with for several months; she was at the top of a long list of 'entertainment' as Trenter called it. Most people in the firm knew about his visitors but said nothing as they feared for their jobs.

Trenter was on the telephone, his feet on the desk. He was having a conversation with one of the firm's managers.

"So they can not come up with the extra funds? Did you tell them that we will pull the plug? Yes, an extra one hundred grand like now! Do you think that I give a shit about their people? They can go under for all I care. They either come up with the cash, or they go, do you understand? Now! I don't care what you think, you do what you are told, or you can clear your desk, get it? Now do it?"

Trenter slammed down the telephone, sat up and smiled to himself. He then went to a wall panel behind his desk and pushed a pin that was hidden from view. There was the sound of a device unlocking and a small panel opened. Inside was a safe. He entered the code then opened the safe door. Inside the safe were several large bundles of fifty-pound notes and papers he had kept secret; contained in the papers were details of people he was blackmailing.

Trenter took out a paper bundle and, leaving the safe open, sat at his desk once more, leafing through the papers. He looked at his watch—he was meeting his latest 'entertainment' in fifteen minutes.

While Trenter sat at his desk, suddenly, he felt his head begin to ache; nothing like a headache he had had previously. He rubbed his temples, but the pain only worsened. Trenter frantically searched his desk drawer for painkillers but could not find any. He stood up, and as he did so, he became aware of a foul smell in the room, just like rotting flesh. He began to wretch, holding his head. The pain increased, his eyes filled with hot stinging tears, he wanted to call out for help, but no sound came from his lips. The pain intensified again.

Staggering to the room's balcony doors, he pushed them open and stood on the threshold, thinking that the fresh air would help. Trenter looked in the glass panels of the doors. What he saw terrified him—holding him around his head was a small figure. The figure was hideous, manlike, with deep red eyes. The demon had long tendril-like claws; the claws Trender could see were penetrating his skull. The demon snarled at Trender and pushed further into his brain, searching for the inner-soul. As he pushed deeper, Trender began to lose any sense of where he was. He staggered forward, holding his head. The demon pushed one last time.

"Theeere," the demon said in a snarling but excited tone. Blood streamed from Trender's nostrils and eye sockets then from his ears. Holding his head but without any control of himself and in unimaginable agony, Trenter staggered to the balustrade. With his hands still holding his head, he was now top-heavy. He fell over the balcony falling eight floors to his death. He landed head first on the pavement below. Witnesses say they saw Trenter walk out onto the balcony where he simply fell forward over it onto the street below.

Chapter 5
Brian

In a smart top-floor penthouse suite within a brand new building development in the centre of the City of Manchester, Brian paced up and down. The apartment was decorated minimally, to say the least, a huge space where no homely warmth was evident. Why should it be? The penthouse was a statement, not a home; it showed off what you get when you approach the top! The only item within the space that had any real meaning for Brian was a small photograph on a very empty shelf unit. The image was of Brian and Ash enjoying themselves in some ski resort. They were both linking arms with their then-girlfriends. Strangely the image had been torn on one side; the side next to Ash where Ash's old girlfriend should have been.

The kitchen was equally as cold and uninviting. A large top-of-the-range American-style refrigerator was empty and unused, and the cooker still had its protective film of plastic applied to the surface. The only evidence that the kitchen had been used were several empty best quality lead crystal whiskey tumblers scattered along the worktop; standing next to the glasses were several empty and part-empty 25-year-old single malt Talisker whiskey bottles. Brian refilled his glass, emptying another bottle. He drank deeply, his hands trembling. Sitting on a stiff new black leather chair, Brian picked up the local newspaper. The headline read:

'CEO of City lawyers killed in a horrific accident'.

The CEO of a reputable city firm of lawyers fell to his death from his office balcony. The Greater Manchester Police have made a statement that they are not looking for anyone else in connection to this case. It would appear from evidence found in an office at the scene that Mr Trenter was involved in the blackmailing of several city traders. This incident does not appear to be connected to another five incidents of apparent accident or suicide, including a Catholic Priest who took his own life by jumping from a Church tower. The Priest, known to locals as Father Gerald, was at the centre of an abuse scandal.

Brian put the paper down, then picked it up again and re-read the front page. He began to laugh a hysterical whimpering laugh. He then took another large deep drink of the Talisker. He stood up and went to the windows which overlook the lit-up city. "I said, scare him, not kill him. Now, what will I do? I'll go away for life. What have you done?"

An almost inaudible cracking voice somewhere in the huge space said, "We did what you were thinking. You did not really want him scared, did you?" The tone was spiteful and also menacing.

"No, you want his job. That has always been your goal. We gave you something you wanted and now you give us something in return. That is how it works. You know how it works. Besides, no one will know it was your doing. He fell, they will find the scale of the corruption and blackmail when they go through his papers."

"But why kill him, why kill him?" Brian almost in tears. "You killed him, *killed!*" he blurted out from between clenched teeth, throwing the glass across the room where it hit the wall and smashed into a thousand sharp shards of glistening crystal, the Talisker staining the bare clinical white wall surface on contact. Hidden out of sight in the darkest recess within the large room, a dark pulsating slime dripped from within the wall, pulsating as it travelled downwards. From this spot came a reply delivered in a cool chilling rasp, *"Yes* and we also have his soul, along with the rest of them."

Brian then said in a panicked voice, "What about Ash? You said nothing about harming him. What do you want with him? He is my only friend, please don't harm him. I will call him and tell him not to come." Brian picked up his mobile telephone and began to push down the numbers. In a flash, his mobile telephone seemed to be torn from his hand and was sent flying to the other side of the room.

A terrible voice sneered and hissed at Brian, "Fool, do you think that you can go back on your word? Do you honestly believe that you can undo what you started? Do you think that you can stop us now? well, do you?" The last couple of words seemed to punch Brian in the head as he reeled backwards from the chair he was sitting in.

"You will do what you are told, do you understand? Answer me, do you understand?"

In a weak voice, Brian said, "Yes."

"This is the price you pay for letting us into your life. You knew what was involved. Wealth, prestige, success, you wanted it all and now you whimper like a child. Pathetic creature, get up and prepare for your invited guest, he approaches."

Chapter 6
M6 Motorway

Continuing his journey southwards through the Highlands, along Loch Lomond and then through Glasgow, Ash thought about what Brian could have done and how he could assist. Yes, the call was out of the blue, but the content of the message, "I have done something terrible." what was all that about? Ash was aware of the ambition Brian craved. He also knew that Brian could be blunt, direct and to the point, also quite self-opinionated, even rude, but Brian was confident, tough and strong-willed, so why did he sound like he had lost his control?

These thoughts had no answers yet and so Ash thought about his encounter earlier that day. "Was it real?" he said to himself, "Did I really speak with my grandmother?"

"Yes, I did! But how, why, what has changed in my life in twenty-four hours to merit firstly Brian and then my gran? What is going on?" he asked himself. His attention was returned sharply as he was flashed from behind by a car wanting to use the second lane of the A74 dual carriageway that he had drifted into. "Shit, I must concentrate!" Putting the questions aside for the time being, Ash began unconsciously practicing what his grandmother had told him. Finding a thought that made him really happy, he could feel the emotion building up in the core of his body. He carefully let the feeling generate outwards until he felt a warm, tingling sensation cover his whole body. Ash practiced again and again; it seemed to come naturally. Even as he thought of the pleasant notion, his body seemed to react and almost immediately he was tingling all over.

His journey continued: he was now on the M6 Southbound. The light was fading fast and the twilight cast interesting shadows on the verges. Shapes seemed to come to life, even chase after him.

"I'm getting tired, that's all."

Darkness came quickly as Ash continued his journey. The roads were particularly quiet, he thought. The Northbound traffic was almost bumper to bumper as he glanced across the carriageway, then without warning, something darted from the shadows straight into his path. Ash could not see what it was, some sort of animal.

"Hold on, an animal, it was standing on two twisted legs!"

Ash slammed on the car brakes as he was going to collide with the figure. At the last second, as he was braking hard, the figure vanished. All Ash could think about were the deep-set sort of eyes; they blazed deep brown-red.

Ash pulled onto the hard shoulder, shaking with fright. "What the hell was that?" he said to himself, "Did I just nod off or something?"

Ash sat for a couple of minutes on the hard shoulder. He was then aware of flashing blue lights in his rear mirror; after a second, a tall police officer was standing at the driver's door.

"Good evening, sir; we saw you brake very hard and stop here. Are you ok, not sick, sir?"

The officer seemed genuinely concerned.

"I am sorry, officer, it has been a long journey. I thought something ran into the carriageway and braked. Did you see it?"

The officer gave a weak smile and said, "No sir, nothing ran into the road. We were right behind you: tiredness probably, why not pull off at the next services? They are only a couple of miles away. Get a coffee and perhaps a power nap."

"Thank you, officer. I will do just that."

The police officer returned to his vehicle and pulled out into the carriageway; Ash followed. The services were only two minutes drive away. Ash indicated left and stopped his car in the large car park in front of MacDonald's. He sat in his car for a while.

"Am I going mad? I did see that thing run out in front of me, and it stared at me. Those eyes, what was it?" Ash said to himself. Settling himself, he walked the short few paces to the takeaway. Walking into the space, it seemed quiet. He could see only a couple of people sitting down: a family, what looked like a lorry driver, some younger kids and an older thin balding man. He gave Ash a thin half-smile when their eyes met; Ash nodded and went to the counter. The assistant was a fresh-faced young girl, probably about seventeen years old. She smiled at Ash and said, "Can I help, sir? You look like you just seen a ghost," in a jolly sort of way. Ash caught a glimpse of his reflection in a mirror; he noticed that he was looking pale and ashen. He said, "Yes, something ran out into the carriageway, gave me a fright!"

She replied, "Yes, we do get small deer running across the motorways. I'm surprised more aren't killed. Are you ready to order, sir?" Ash ordered a large coffee and a Big Mac meal. He sat down opposite the thin man. As he ate his meal, he was aware that the thin man was watching him; Ash, however, was too hungry to respond in any way and very quickly had eaten the burger and fries. He was about to take a sip of his coffee when the thin man came and sat next to him

"Can you help me? I need to get to Manchester. Are you going that way?"

The man's voice was not very clear; it sounded like

he was suffering from laryngitis or something. Ash also noticed that the man was not so clean and that there was a foul smell coming from him. Ash being Ash however said without thinking "Yes, I am on my way to Manchester, no problem."

"What have I just done?" Ash said to himself. "I'll wait outside," the man said.

Finishing off his cup of coffee, Ash said goodbye and went to his car; waiting next to his car was the strange man. Ash thought, "How did he know which was my car?" Thinking no more about that fact, Ash greeted the man and invited him to get into the car. The immediate issue for Ash was the smell coming from this man; not quite a dirty smell rather than a decaying rotting sort of smell. Ash wound down his window slightly. Pressing the transmitting key, the car started and they moved off. Ash thought to himself, 'Thank God Manchester is only several junctions away; this smell is terrible!'

Ash said, "How remiss of me, I am Ash, good to meet you, and your name?" The man was looking directly ahead and made a noise, again it sounded like he had an issue with his throat.

"Sorry, I missed that, but you sound like you have a terrible sore throat; names aren't important anyway." The man made another noise, continuing to look ahead. There was an uneasy silence for a while, so Ash turned on the radio; soft classical music began to fill the silent void within the car. Traffic was still light travelling south but the north carriageway was nose to tail. Ash glanced to his left where he saw his passenger. His head was slightly downward facing and he was muttering to himself.

Ash had witnessed similar behaviour through his job, dealing with the unfortunate individuals who found themselves destitute and homeless. The worse for consuming cheap booze or using drugs, they would sit in the street with their heads down muttering to themselves, and so the behaviour of this strange man sitting next to Ash was not a surprise. Ash felt pity and took away his gaze.

Chapter 7
Daphne

Several minutes passed when Ash felt a slight headache begin. He thought it was simply tiredness; however, the headache intensified. Ash thought he could hear the muttering noises getting louder. He again glanced to his left. The strange man was rocking back and forth, his lips moving fast. The muttering was getting more intense and louder. Ash felt his headache become sharper, he began to feel nauseous and his senses became confused. Ash then realised that this sensation was beginning to grow. He felt a warmth develop in his core; he tried to focus on it but the nausea feeling developed into retching. The stranger next to him appeared to move so fast back and forth that it became a blur, or was this simply Ash reacting to the imminent throwing up episode? Once again braking hard and pulling his car onto the hard shoulder, Ash opened his door and vomited. Another wave of nausea came. This time he staggered out of the car to the hedge verge and threw up. His eyes watered continuously, blurring his vision. He did not hear the person approach him from behind, neither could he see what was happening in the front of his car.

Another stomach retch and hot vomit covered the hedgerow and his shoes. He then felt a hand on his on his left shoulder. Ash swung about with surprise. His eyes were still blurred with fresh hot stinging tears, the taste of bile in his mouth, but the touch seemed to comfort him. Ash gathered himself but still could not focus. He was aware of lights approaching from behind, then the person standing behind of him said, "You are safe now, the danger has passed, focus on your inner feeling Ash, focus." Believing that this was the same motorway policeman Ash said, "Thank you, officer," then Ash was aware that he was alone standing on the hard shoulder.

He regained clear vision and looked behind him for the police car—there was no vehicle. He turned and looked at his car. In the headlight beam of his vehicle Ash saw something dart out of sight into the darkness. It appeared to be running on twisted legs. "Not that animal thing again!" Ash said to himself. Returning to the driver's side of his car, Ash lent down and was about to apologise to the strange man, but the man was not there. The passenger's door was slightly open; the stranger was gone, so was the foul smell. Ash noticed that on the passenger seat, dribbling down the plastic covering was a dark reddish-brown slime. It was pulsing, then it too vanished. Ash sat heavily on the driver's seat and exhaled. He then took in a large breath of air. There was an aroma he was aware of; it was the beautiful scent of the 'Daphne' shrub. It soothed Ash and all at once was gone. Ash thought, "I will be so happy when I get to Brian's, I have seen too much tonight."

He continued his journey into Manchester.

Chapter 8
The Penthouse

In the penthouse in the centre of Manchester city, Brian poured himself another large whiskey. He sat heavily on a chair, muttering to himself. The side of his face was deep red with what looked like a claw mark. He then became aware of another presence in the large room. He didn't even look to the dark corner where voices began to talk in a crude, jerky, sneering tone.

"He had help! And he has talent!"

"What do you expect, fool? He is the one, he has been selected. Do you think this is random? You're more a fool than I thought," rasped the other. "Patience, patience, soon enough he will be here and our Master will be pleased with you, then you can join my rank. But go it alone again, and I will not assist you; you will burn forever, get it?"

In a voice that sounded like it had a sore throat, a weaker voice said, "Yes, master."

Ash continued his journey, arriving in Manchester city at around two-thirty am. His satnav had taken him directly to the apartments where Brian waited, nervous and terrified. Ash followed the parking sign and came to a large iron gate. To the driver's side of the gate was a box panel with a blue button. Ash pressed the button and the gate opened, allowing Ash to park his car underneath the apartment block. The parking space was designated for two vehicles belonging to the penthouse suite, and next to the parking area was a private lift for the exclusive use of the penthouse owner.

Ash pressed an intercom button; after a couple of seconds, an automated voice said, "Enter." The lift door opened and Ash stepped into a smoked glass-lined lift. The lift door closed silently and without any effort, it carried Ash to the top floor. In silence, the lift door opened onto a large marble- floored inner reception hallway. It seemed strange as there was nothing on the walls, no ornaments, nothing, the space was barren and cold.

Ash stepped over the threshold and looked straight ahead; the smell of hot body odour and whiskey met his senses. He walked a short distance along the bare hallway into a generous sized room with high ceilings. From the large window, the yellow-orange glow of the city could be seen. Sitting in a black chair with his head in his hands was Brian. There was no greeting, just a slight gesture with a hand which Ash took to mean, *'Hi, and welcome to my home.'* Brian leaned forward and took his glass of whisky. He indicated the glass to Ash; Ash said, "No thanks."

Looking more closely at Brian, Ash saw that the clothes he was wearing were stained and creased as though they had been slept in. He was unshaven, and his hair was dishevelled, but it was Brian's eyes; they were wide, staring, bloodshot eyes. Brian looked up towards Ash and said, "Thanks for coming." Ash said, "Brian, what the hell is this all about? You look terrible. What have you done?"

Ash pulled another black leather chair and sat in front of Brian. Now that he was closer, Ash could see just how dreadful Brian looked; he also noted the angry red marks across his face. It was also apparent that Brian had not washed for some time, the smell of stale body odour was so bad; his fingernails were long and yellow and filthy. What had happened to the sharp, smart immaculate lawyer, Ash had last seen?

Brian pushed a fine crystal whisky tumbler half-full of amber liquid across the marble floor to Ash. Brian then raised his glass to Ash. Picking the glass up, Ash returned the gesture and quietly said, "Cheers," Something inside of Ash told him not to drink from the glass; he ignored the sensation in preference to the pity he had for a friend who was clearly in serious trouble. The liquid tasted bitter, but Ash swallowed it all the same, all of it in one go. He thought the bitter taste was a result of his earlier vomiting episode.

Within seconds of taking the drink, Ash felt his mind sway: *'tiredness after the excitement of the journey,'* he thought. Then the inside of his mouth dried out; he could not gather any saliva to swallow. Ash slumped backwards into the large black chair. All sensation in his hands began to leave. A painful numbness travelled up his arms, also from his feet and legs. Fear gripped him; blind terror engulfed him. His eyes were set on Brian. Ash attempted to speak; nothing passed his lips. "What is he doing, why, oh, God, what is he doing?" Locked into his mind, the only thing Ash was capable of was seeing and thinking. The seeing was terrifying as Ash watched Brian slowly rise out of his chair, his bloodshot eyes intensely staring at Ash, a snarl on his lips as Brian moved ever closer to Ash's set face.

"This is all your bastard fault, your fault! I would have been someone if it wasn't for you. You were the special one, I was always in your shadow. You were the smart bastard one; I always had to keep up, sitting up for hours reading over and over again and again, just to be able to answer those stupid bastard questions. You could rest while I worked. You always got the good looker. I got the seconds. Then you went and moved to that god-forsaken bastard north. You left me behind with no one. Do you know what it is like to have no one, do you?" Brian's voice had risen to a hysterical whining. He continued: "You bastard went and left me, so when they offered friendship, I took it. I was promised things: promotions, money, women, yes, the life I had always wanted, given to me by them, and for what, *YOU!* That's for what, you, they exalted you they wanted you, not me, you!"

Brian sunk to his knees weeping, the words almost unintelligible: "You, they wanted you, not me, never me. Oh God, Ash, they killed Trenter. I only wanted them to scare him, but they killed him, and I think they want to kill you. I've set you up Ash; God forgive me, I've killed you! Get out of here NOW, run as fast as you can. Go. Go!"

As the full horror struck Ash, his head throbbed in fear.

"God, who has he set me up with, what criminals has he got mixed up with, and what do they want with me, what have I done?"

Realising that he had been drugged, terror threatened to overwhelm his senses. His mind's focus became blurred and raced. He so wanted to get up and run, but he was fixed in place: not able to move, not able to speak, just able to breathe, his lungs just about able to take in just enough air. He felt as if he was sinking into quicksand. He felt huge pressure pushing down on him, and only his eyes were visible from the surface. Ash screamed inwardly, a scream that knew that death was imminent.

Chapter 9
The Reward

From the dark space in the corner of the room, there was movement, then a voice. The voice was mocking the last words spoken by Brian, "Run Ash, run, go, go," then in a sneering, cackled, husky, almost sore throat tone, the voice spoke again.

"He wants you to run Ash, but you can't, can you? No, you can't even speak, your best friend here has seen to that! Yes, your best friend, how does that feel? To know you have been betrayed—oh no, you can't speak, silly me, but you can watch, yes, you can watch your best friend receive his gift from me for allowing us in."

Ash could not see who or where the voice was coming from. His eyes only saw what was directly in front of him, but in an uncanny way, he recognised the voice, the sore throat tone. Then from the edge of his vision came the shape of a man, a thin man, a thin balding man. This man walked on what Ash thought looked like twisted legs! Again Ash's mind raced; he recalled the brief encounters only hours previously. 'How can this be happening?' he thought. Then in full view, Ash saw the twisted form of what looked human standing in front of him. The thin man bent down and put his face next to Ash's, eye to eye. Ash was forced to look directly into the other's eyes, but they were not eyes: they were deep sockets of blackness. Deep within the darkness, Ash could see fire, a deep red burning, then he said, "Oh yes, it is me, surprise! And now witness your *bestest* friend's reward for his hard selfless, oh did I say selfless? I mean his selfish self-centred desires."

The words were spat out of this vile creature with abject contempt. Brian, who was still on his knees weeping uncontrollably, then stopped when he heard mention of his reward. His selfishness and greed for himself put away the brief concern he had for Ash—now the focus was on him. "My reward, for me, a reward just for me," he said with a hysterical laugh, "A reward for me, for me, a reward for me". It was clear that Brian had lost his mind, swaying from hysterical laughter to weeping. Brian got to his feet and stumbled to where Ash had him in full view. He said to the thin balding man, "What have you got for me? What reward?" Brian had a sort of grin on his lips and expectation in his wild eyes. "Give it to me then, my reward, give it to me, now!" he shouted, his voice getting louder and demanding. *"NOW, NOW!"* He said directly into the face of the thin man.

Ash watched as the thin man seemed to shimmer in and out of focus. The snarl on his lips grew, the dark eye sockets began to blaze, and his hands altered shape. Where there were thin fingers, now claw-like spindly tendrils appeared. Brian did not seem to be aware of these changes. He was so focused on the imminent delivery of his reward that he simply stood looking vacant.

"Do it now; it is yours for the taking, join my rank brother," a second voice spoke. Ash could not see where the other voice came from.

"Take it, what is left of it anyway, let him know the cost of letting us in, give him his just reward!"

"Yes, Master," the thin man said in a terrible voice. The demon straightened and, in the direct view of Ash, took hold of Brian's head. Brian attempted to pull away from the grasp. A look of terror suddenly struck Brian as he felt one of the tendrils enter his head at his temple. Brian screamed in agony as a second tendril entered the other temple, blood trickling down both sides of his face, then the demon sunk all tendrils into Brian's head. A blood-curdling scream shot from Brian's mouth together with hot steaming fresh blood.

"Not so quickly, my brother, let him suffer. That's it, slowly, deeply. Remind him what real pain is."

Ash watched in horror, not able to respond, not able to vomit at the sight of the grotesque assault on his friend. Then briefly, he sensed the subtle scent of *Daphne;* the aroma vanished as swiftly as it had arrived. In that instant, the demon quickly glanced at Ash, then as quickly resumed its probing, searching for its prize.

Ash felt a brief feeling of comfort; then he could no longer hear the screams coming from Brian. "Concentrate, gather your inner-feelings, create your shield."

Then the sound of screaming returned. Ash focused his inner-self, and without any more effort, he was aware that the sensation was returning to his body, from the core radiating outwards, slowly, subtly. Ash could feel the poison being driven out of his blood. Sweat began to leak from his body. The poison was leaving him, but he was still stricken, terrified and sickened by the sight of what was taking place in front of his eyes.

Brian's screams subsided, to be replaced by whimpering groans. Brian's feet were no longer on the polished marble flooring: they were a couple of inches off the ground, twitching occasionally, thrashing wildly. Blood was now escaping from his eye sockets. Thick grey liquid dripped from his nostrils. The demon's tendrils were completely inside of Brian's head, yet he was still alive. Then the demon shouted in a dreadful voice, "Yes, Yes!"

The demon withdrew its tendril-like claws from Brian's head. Brian fell onto the marble floor with a heavy, sickening thud; hot thick grey and red matter oozed from each temple. Brian's eyes twitched; his legs jerked one way then another. Where his hands were in contact with the marble, they appeared to be melting, turning into black-red blood-slime. His forearms began to melt onto the floor, then the second demon said, "Now for your true reward, hell!" At these words, Brian opened his eyes. Ash could see that in Brian's eyes was inconceivable horror; then in the centre of his eyes, Ash saw blackness growing. In the centre of the blackness was a small fire.

Brian continued to melt into the putrid slime. The final word that escaped his melting mouth was directed at Ash: "You!" Brian's whole body then melted into the black slime and appeared to be absorbed by the marble until nothing remained.

The demon still standing in front of Ash was holding a small, dimly glowing orb in its claws. The demon looked very closely at this glowing matter and said, "His soul is now mine forever, I too will grow and be an equal to you, my brother." Then the demon with one of his tendril-like claws lacerated the front area of his own forehead. The seeping wound exposed a writhing mass of red-black slime. The demon pushed the orb into the opening, which closed straight away. The demon then stood up, shimmering aggressively. The demon's legs straightened, and he appeared to lose some of the age he had. His hair also became fuller. He smirked and said, "Now him!"

Chapter 10
Confrontation

Ash continued to feel more and more sensation returning to him. His lungs inhaled deeper breaths. He was able to move his eyes and felt tingling in his fingers and his legs. Ash was now aware that his inner shield was at its full extent, covering his whole body. He needed little effort to hold it in place; it was simply natural.

Ash was able to move his eyes in the direction of the other voice. He was surprised to see a tall, well-built man. He had long dark hair tied in a ponytail; his skin was also dark, almost Egyptian. He was wearing casual clothes and a leather jacket. His hands, however, were not human-looking, more like bird claws. His eyes were a blaze of intense yellow fire. When he spoke, it was clearer than the other demon and with sarcastic overtones. This demon had an air of superiority about him.

Lunging towards Ash, the smaller demon grabbed hold of Ash's left arm and said, "You're mine," As the demon's claw made contact with Ash's arm, the demon retracted immediately and screamed in intense pain as its claw burst into hot blue flames. The larger demon, at the same moment with unbelievable agility, swung its large claw at the smaller demon, connected with the side of his head and spat out the words, "You dare to offend our Master in this way. It is for our Master to deal with this one, not you!"

It again swung the now huge claw at the smaller demon, sending it backwards across the room. The smaller demon got to its feet, looking at the smouldering stump that remained where it's claw had been. A rage consumed it and it transformed into a contorted animal-like creature, stooped over, standing on two twisted legs. Baring its long dark fangs, it lunged at the larger demon, sinking its teeth into the thigh of the other demon and pulling off a chunk of steaming green flesh. Retracting slightly, both demons now stalked each other. The larger demon had assumed a huge terrifying bear creature form. Its jaw jutted out and was drooling foul acid slime.

"You think you can take me?" the bear demon snarled at the other. "I am your equal now, brother," he replied with contempt.

"Arrogant fool, you know nothing. You believe that soul was worthy, it was empty, yes empty, you are nothing!".

With its focus enraged instantaneously, the bear demon elongated its claws and grabbed hold of the writhing smaller creature. It smashed it against a nearby wall. The smaller demon screamed a horrific scream before again sinking its huge fangs into the exposed limb and ripping at the flesh. The bear demon winced in pain.

The bear-like demon retained its grip on the other and extended its claws which penetrated the smaller body. The small demon cried a hideous gurgling sound.

"Forgive me, forgive me."

There was no reply. The bear demon strengthened its grip on the other. Black slime began to ooze from its eye sockets then the smaller demon spontaneously combusted; green and dirty yellow flames engulfed its entire body. Holding on, the bear demon said in a commanding and dangerous tone, "Return to the lowest ranks, fool." The flames intensified and the smaller demon vanished. The bear demon slowly turned to face Ash, a look of abject contempt on its contorted face. It hissed at him.

Chapter 11
Stand Off

During the confrontation between both demons, Ash was aware that his body was completely free from the poison. He also knew that his inner shield was intensifying; it seemed that he was on autopilot. Watching the horrific scenes unfolding in front of him, Ash now felt less terrified. He felt as if he was observing the whole event from a distance, a safe distance. He felt strong both physically and mentally; he also felt prepared for whatever was to take place next.

Ash looked on almost with amusement as the two demons battled. He said to himself when the smaller demon vanished, "Well, at least that is one less." This thought brought a thin smile to his face. The larger demon hissed at Ash one more time as though he understood what Ash was thinking.

The large sitting room in which the events had taken place was suddenly silent. There was an eerie deafening quiet, a tense and dangerous quiet. The smell of rotting and burnt flesh hung in the air. To Ash, his senses were telling him that this was the quiet before the storm. "Who was this demon's Master?" Ash asked himself. "When was it going to show up?" he thought.

Ash considered what had taken place over the last twelve hours or so: the call from Brian, Brian the smartest toughest lawyer he knew, now gone, murdered by demons! The meeting with his deceased grandmother who instructed him to protect himself, well, it seemed to work; the smaller demon demonstrated that. Ash thought about the strange encounters on the motorway, the animal-like creature that darted into his path, then the thin man at the services, who just happened to be the small demon. What was all of this leading to?

Ash got up onto his feet and once again took in the scene. A calmness had taken over his emotions. The demon was standing near a dark corner of the room. It seemed to be speaking at the wall. Ash could not hear any words but heard sounds and saw gesticulations. The wall surface was pulsating; black slime was dripping downwards from cracks in the pristine white paint. The cracks were getting larger, more black slime began to pour out of the widening cracks, then smoke or steam began to escape, and deep in the cracks, Ash saw glowing green-yellow fire.

In a matter-of-fact tone, Ash said, "Well, I'll be away then." He began to walk towards the hallway and the lift, when without turning, the demon said, "Stay exactly where you are, we're not finished with you!" The statement was spoken in a calm, almost friendly manner. "Please take a seat," said the demon. "No, actually, I think I would like to leave now." Ash sensed the tension build. His shield automatically strengthened, he became ultra-alert, and then with a cracking, snarling voice, the demon said, "Sit." The air in the room cracked at the command. The demon turned to face Ash. Its face was contorted, its thin lips sagging at the edges of its mouth and the fire in its eyes blazed.

"No, as a matter of fact, I will not sit. I am leaving now!" In a flash, the demon lashed out with its evil force. A pulse of hatred flew across the space between them, the demon's face flashed with contemptuous wickedness and it spat out, *"SIT DOWN!"*

As if anticipating this action, Ash faced the demon. He saw the evil force approach him; it seemed to be travelling in slow motion. Ash looked at the energy; he could see raw hatred bound together with the screaming souls of this demon's previous victims, faces coming in and out of focus, all contorted in agony, all wanting to harm Ash.

Ash put up his hand and said in a voice he had never spoken in previously, *"NO."* The command boomed from him; instantaneously, the demons force was repelled. Travelling back at it much faster than it had left it, the pulse hit the demon full-on, sending it flying across the marble floor. A look of unbelievable surprise and shock on its hideous face, the demon remained stuck, unable to move on the point of impact with the floor.

Ash seemed to be slightly taken aback by his actions. It was as if his autopilot recognised the level of danger and the method of assault and responded in the same way, clearly taking the demon by absolute surprise. He then said to the demon, "And this time I will leave, and might I suggest that you do the same." From the ever-growing cracks in the wall came a sound. A cackling wicked laugh escaped from the wall into the huge room, then in a terrifying snarling voice from inside the wall came the words, *"Yesss, Yesss,* you do have talent. Interesting; however, your confidence will be short-lived, boy."

Chapter 12
The Master

Cracks in the white walls opened further, a figure casually stepped through the opening in the wall.

Surrounded by some sort of vapour appeared a small skeletal man. The slime surrounding the figure pulsed, it was alive, writhing in dark light as if you were looking into a phosphorescent dark water. The figure had no real facial features apart from the eyes, which were pools of glowing darkest green, almost black with vertical slits for pupils. Inside of the pupil's slits was a red fire burning. Ash could not take his gaze away from these eyes. They seemed to compel him.

"And you wanted to leave the party I so carefully arranged for you, boy."

The words were spoken with the utmost hatred. He said, *"NOW, SIT."* his eyes flashed, and Ash found himself being forced backwards and thrust into the black leather chair.

"Oh no, I'm afraid that your talent can not affect me. In time it will be I who will show you what power is!"

The Lord demon scanned the room and said to the other demon, "You have done well, now stand at my side while I take what belongs to me." The other demon stood up, slightly shaken still. Its skin or covering appeared to be smouldering. It gingerly moved and stood slightly behind the Master. "Thank you, Master," it said in a subservient tone.

Ash, still calm, collected his thoughts. He asked himself, "Who is this? What do I have that he wants?" As if Ash had spoken out loud, the Demon Lord replied, "You will know in good time what you have that I want. You will know in good time who I am." The demon Lord then turned to face his subordinate and he began to communicate with him. The other simply nodded in response.

Chapter 13
Demon Lord

A sh attempted to get out of the chair. He pushed his will, but nothing happened. He tried again: it seemed to him that the more he flexed his will the more pressure was exerted against him.

"You are wasting your time, boy. The more you struggle, the more I pin you down. It is simple, when will you learn to accept your fate?"

There was an inevitability in that statement. Ash realised that he was in trouble; however, panic and terror did not reappear, instead, his whole self became calmer. Ash again seemed to be observing this whole crazy event from a distance.

He thought about the words the demon Lord had said. Something struck a chord: the reference to a 'party,' that was it. During all of the events that had unfolded in the last twenty-four hours, Ash had completely forgotten that it was his thirtieth birthday today. Ash had never taken any notice of birthdays. They just happened, that was all. Could this be a coincidence? Is this what the demon Lord was talking about, his party, my party?

Ash pushed his will again, only this time he tried to keep the effort silent. He wondered if he could hide the effort from this demon Lord. Feeling his shield touching the pressure that now held him down he pushed. He began to make progress as the pressure lessened, furthermore, there was no reaction from the demon Lord apart from a quick sideward glance towards him. Ash smothered his efforts again and this time he felt the weight lighten even more, so much so that he felt that he could quite easily escape, but against two demons, his inner-self was screaming caution.

Feeling more confident, Ash decided that he wanted to understand more about the situation he was in. He spoke to the demon Lord: "Ok then, what is it that you want so very much from me?"

"My, your arrogance is breathtaking. What I want has belonged to me since the day you were born, boy. Oh, I take it that this has never been explained to you, not even by that interfering bitch of a grandmother of yours!"

Ash was momentarily taken aback at the reference to his grandmother. He said, "You knew my grandmother?" The demon Lord straightened and walked towards Ash, his eyes ablaze, the movement within his slimy skin shifting around very fast. As he walked his body twitched as if he was allergic to something in the room. Then he said, "Know your grandmother? Know your grandmother?" spitting the words out like water thrown onto hot coals.

"I killed the bitch, ah, you had no idea. How brave, they have kept you in the dark all this time. It is quite simple, boy: you have something I want, your gran tried to protect you from me, she got in the way, so I killed her and took her soul."

Ash said, "But you didn't get what you wanted from me did you, you evil filth? You failed to get that which you covet most, didn't you? Didn't you?" Tears welled up in Ash's eyes as the full truth surfaced: this monster had murdered his grandmother.

Mocking Ash the demon Lord said, "Crying for your little weak grandmother are we? You are pitiful, weak, not worthy and her death was so simple, as will yours be!"

Turning to the other demon the Lord commanded,

"Take him, put him on the altar, now."

Chapter 14
The Altar

In the centre of the room, in front of the oozing slime wall appeared a red hot smouldering altar. It had the appearance of cooling magma; flames shot out of cracks in the surface. On the top of the hot stone were shackles; these too glowed red hot. There was also a large knife on the slab; this glowed with a green and yellow fire.

On seeing this Ash froze. He now realised that this was for him, he was being sacrificed, for what he thought? The under demon approached Ash cautiously. Ash pushed all fears from himself and waited. The demon gathered its will and forced it around Ash. The effort required was huge. Ash waited until the demon showed a slight sign of stress at holding its will then he released his own inner will. The effect was instantaneous: the under demon howled as its whole body suddenly began to smoulder. The smouldering turned into flames, intense blue flames engulfed it, and it screamed an insane sound as the blue flames became brighter. No longer the large form, it started to shrink.Its howls of agony were deafening, but Ash maintained the effort. Then all at once the blue light grew brighter, starlight entombed the demon, and the demon was gone.

Cackling a few paces away, the demon Lord clapped his slimy hands together.

"Bravo, bravo, a quaint little trick, one might say 'childlike', but you are no match for me boy!"

The demon Lord raised a limb, it's face twisted into an ugly smile, it then released its power directly at Ash.

The pulse of power knocked Ash backwards but he remained on his feet. Ash was completely surrounded by green crackling and hissing energy. He pushed his own will against his adversary's trying as he could to repel the force of will but made no impact. The demon Lord said, "Weakness, weakness, let me spell it out to you boy, you are weak, I am strong. It is simple; your soul is mine for that taking. How dare you think that you are my equal! You are nothing, *nothing.*"

Ash was lifted off his feet and carried in an invisible cocoon toward the crackling altar. The demon Lord was enjoying every second. He cackled as Ash once again pushed as hard as he could against the will of this monster. Nothing happened. "Mine, all mine," came the unholy voice of the demon.

Ash was thrown down on the altar. The contact between him and the boiling rock created an abundance of sparks. As soon as Ash touched the altar he was restrained by thin tendrils that came from within the altar, his wrists and ankles were held firm. Ash continued to push his will out, attempting to free himself. Realisation struck Ash, he was actually restrained on a piece of molten rock and had red hot tendrils surrounding his wrists and ankles, yet he felt no heat, no discomfort. The shield that Ash had generated was protecting him from the worst of the red hot rock and shackles.

At his side the demon Lord said, "You do possess talent. I have not seen this level in any other human, interesting that it is only on your death bed that you should find this quality! Only on your death bed will you fully understand what it is that I will take from you. To have a soul such as yours will indeed propel me even further. I will be given legions to command. This is what your dear gran wanted to avoid, this is what she died for, to protect you from me, but she failed, she failed boy. I also took her pathetic soul, and now you will follow her. By the way boy, you will spend the rest of time smouldering in the depths of hell, where you will do my bidding, yes my bidding. Now you will die!"

The demon Lord grabbed hold of the knife from the altar and raised it above his head. With his gnarled hand, the demon Lord summoned a sharp-pointed single claw to appear. He placed the claw against Ash's forehead. "Yess, there it is." The demon Lord attempted to push his claw into the side of Ash's temple; although the skin was depressed, the surface tension remained intact. The demon Lord said sarcastically, "Try as you will, you are weakening. It is only a matter of time before I get into your head, only time."

The demon Lord then drew down the knife swiftly, penetrating Ash's stomach. At the same time the single claw broke the skin on his temple. In a hissing call of success the demon Lord said, *"Yesssss,* at last, now you will feel my presence inside you and you will perish!"

Ash could feel the knife digging deep into his flesh. He felt the pressure of the pin sharp claw entering his temple but he did not feel any pain. He once again felt as if he were an observer of this violation. He could also sense the euphoric self- congratulation the demon was now showing. Ash knew that he was about to die and simply said to himself, "I am sorry I failed."

Chapter 15
Grandmother

*"*Get your foul evil claw out of my grandson's head, you evil monster!"And with a gesture from the woman standing in front of the demon Lord, his claw involuntarily retracted. The knife was ejected at the same time and flew across the room. Ash's grandmother immediately sent another forceful blow at the demon, this pushed it several feet away from Ash.

The demon Lord steadied itself and faced the small woman, tilting its head from one side to the other as if looking for something. Then it stood quite still. "You, you, how is this possible, I killed you, I took your soul!"

The demon Lord screamed at Ash's grandmother. She stood between the demon Lord and Ash facing the demon Lord. Still in her simple blue dress, her silver-grey hair shimmered with intense bright blue light. She maneuvered closer to the alter, all of the time watching the demon. A touch from her hand on the tendrils binding her grandson immediately released their restraint of Ash. With no effort at all, she lifted her grandson and placed him onto the marble floor. Blood began to seep from the wounds in his stomach and temples. Ash felt weak but still confident.

"I killed you, you bitch. How is this possible?" the demon said in a dangerous tone of voice.

Ash's grandmother replied in a calm, soft voice, "Your confidence is clouded, your self congratulation misplaced your recollection corrupted by vile self adoration. Yes, we fought, but no, you did not kill me. I died before you killed me." The demon retorted, "Impossible, I took your soul, I caused your death, this cannot be so!" Ash's grandmother replied, "I gave myself to save Ash. I was weakened by our encounter, as were you. That is why you have waited so long to return. No, you did not take my soul even though you ravaged my head searching for it. My soul is quite safe, thank you. What you took was an empty shell. My soul had just left so it seemed to you like it was still present. Believe me, you took nothing, you failed more than you can possibly know. I however took something of yours—I took your intentions with me, stored safely and out of your sight. I have known all along what your intentions have been. You are a vile creature even for hell, your deeds will not go unpunished and as for your aspirations to command legions, so sorry old Lord, but you have quite frankly failed!"

The last remarks from Ash's grandmother enraged the demon. His wildness became insanity, the contents of his body began to boil in rage, his eyes widened at the significance of what he had just learned. Black slime covered the floor around him. The altar flickered and melted back into the cracks in the walls.

"You and your vile underlings have crossed the very lines that were set up to keep your monstrosities from taking place. Using vulnerable humans to gain access to their domain is forbidden, but it seems that you even wish to ignore your ultimate being, who, I can tell you is not best pleased with your actions. I do believe that you are heading to that place that even demons dread, purgatory. You have brought this all upon yourself and now you will pay".

Before Ash's grandmother could react, the demon Lord cast the full force of his will at her, sending her flying through the air. She landed heavily and was winded, the blue iridescence flickered. Ash stood tall and darted at great speed to his grandmother. He extended his will around her; she said in a quiet voice "Thank you, my dear grandson, but that will not be necessary." She smiled at Ash and got to her feet. Ash realised that his grandmother was not a ghost—she was real; he had just touched her.

The demon Lord stomped towards her, gathering his will as he got closer and closer. He said through his clenched mouth, "You are weak, you are of no consequence to me. I will lead the legions and you will be no more. Weak little granny, letting your little boy watch as you are destroyed once and for all!" The demon Lord focused his evil will and unleashed it at her. She said, "You are too blind to see, aren't you? You believe that I am defenceless, alone, well you are wrong, oh so wrong."

At that moment another person was in the room, a big man. Ash took a second glance: "How could this be?" he said to himself. Standing in front of the demon Lord was the figure of the policeman who had assisted Ash on the motorway.

"Father," Ash's grandmother said, "You took your time." The demon Lord, realising that he was now outnumbered, raised his will once more. Instead of releasing it at the woman, his aim was straight at Ash. Ash was prepared: the terrifying force was released from the demon Lord, Ash stood his ground. He waited. Once again Ash saw the energy that was released at him travel in slow motion. Ash could feel the intense evil, hear abject hatred contained within the energy. Ash looked into the eyes of the demon Lord; he felt a hint of pity for it.

In the same moment, Ash's great-grandfather raised a clenched fist, Ash observed that the fist had become the size of a football. The fist struck out so fast and with such force at the demon Lords head that on contact, distorted and flattened it, spraying red and black slime in all directions. The area surrounding the demon shimmered and fractured. Everything was now happening in slow motion.

The energy pulse from the demon Lord struck Ash, he simply absorbed it. The demon Lord regained its form following the punch to the head and looked at Ash and his great-grandfather, horror and confusion written on its features.

Then Ash released energy back at the demon Lord. This time the energy within Ash connected with that of the demon Lord; the result was instantaneous. Slowly the demon Lord looked at the three others, it seemed that the demon Lord had a look of regret on its features, it howled. The covering of its body split open allowing its contents to escape, steaming black slime poured from every crack in the demon, more howling and then in one explosion, darkness enveloped the demon Lord and it was gone.

Chapter 16
Answers

All of the slime on the walls retracted, the cracks in the walls repaired, the air cleared of the smell of rotten flesh and sulphur to be replaced with the sweet perfume of Daphne. Peace returned to the space. Out of the window the sun began to rise; beautiful orange shafts of light illuminated the interior white walls of the penthouse. It was over

"There is nothing more to be gained from staying here. If you leave now, Ash, nobody will have known you were here. We can get rid of any evidence; the neighbour will think that Brian simply went away. In fact get back into your car and return to the Highlands. We will meet you on Rannach Moor, where we can talk further. You did well son," his grandmother said. A nod of agreement came from his great grandfather.

Ash travelled through the rest of the morning. He felt no tiredness. In fact, he was not sure how he felt. As Ash approached the Highlands, he felt that he was once more home again. He opened the car windows and the fresh Highland air filled the space. He took several deep breaths; it seemed to feed his soul. Loch Lomond to his right, Ash marvelled at the wild untamed beauty of his homeland. Passing through Tyndrum, he stopped at the best fish and chip shop. He realised he was starving; he had not eaten anything for hours. Feeling refreshed and full of delicious food he continued on his journey.

When Ash topped the road onto Rannoch Moor he pulled over into a small car park and got out of the car. He walked to where the vista was so huge it created emotions in those who appreciated the vista. A great expanse of wilderness, high mountains enrobed in cloud. Wild deer and hare together with the mighty eagles. He took several more welcome deep breaths of air. He felt at peace.

Ash was aware that he was not alone. "Grandmother," he said. "Oh, don't be so formal, gran or nan will do. What about you, dad?" she said. In a deep, rich Scottish voice Ash's great grandfather said, "Pop, will suffice."

"Well, I am glad that has been sorted out." She gave both men a long kindly look. "Ash, you will no doubt have many questions. Perhaps I can simply say that you are and have always been a very special boy, not simply to your family, but to the world. You and a handful of others have special gifts; however, because of these gifts, you are targets for those who would steal them and kill you at any cost. Our family have been honoured over the ages to receive such gifts. You cannot display them out in the open, they are subtle invisible gifts: kindness, an acute ability to see right from wrong, good from evil. That, by the way, is why you chose the route you chose: you are a helper, you see the hurt in others and you help. Even you do not know just how much you have helped others. That is out of sight to all of us. You will discover more about your gift and how you can use it, but seen from other planes you shine like a bright star and therefore, you are a target. You are a great danger to others who seek more unsavoury traits. Ash, there is a war, it has been so almost since the beginning of the arrival of mankind. You have already tasted the bitter pill, the evil and despair. For you Ash this is the start of a path that you must travel, a path that is dangerous. You must stay on guard from this moment on. Are you with me so far?" Ash replied, "Yes, I think so gran." She said, "Good."

Ash continued: "Gran, you gave your life for me, you saved me from the demons. You have given everything for me!" She replied, "Ash, Ash, my dear, dear son, what I did I would do time and again, and no, it was not me who saved you from the demons, it was you Ash, it was you. I simply gave you guidance, it is you who has the talent and that is why the demon Lord wanted your soul. You have a rare and special gift. From the moment you were born you were selected. We knew that you were special and we were selected to aid you, but inside of course you already know that. The job choice you made for instance, it shows that you are compelled to help others. A time will come when the gift you have will make a huge difference, a difference to many Ash. There is and has always been a war between good and evil. You are part of that war, you have demonstrated that you are worthy and you are linked to a group of special people who will be pushed to the limit. Our input is of no consequence, we simply nudged you in the right direction."

Ash said, "But gran, you came in and saved the day with Pop."

"Appearances can be deceiving. I had to time our arrival; that is all. I knew when the demon Lord was at his weakest. Don't be fooled Ash, he is exceptionally powerful. A demon Lord is a very cunning and powerful adversary. He could have got rid of us with a thought, but he was focused on you. I could not stop him using the knife, I had to let him penetrate your head, as at that point he was fully committed to you and at his most vulnerable. No, Ash it was you, I simply made it look like I had domination over him. He was blinded to his weakness, his need for your soul blinded everything else and his self centred applause occupied his attention. So when I arrived I was able to offset him, that is all, it was you who saved me Ash, my beloved boy, it was your talent and ability to love."

Ash said, "What happened when Pop arrived?" Gran said, "Again, Ash, this was a calculated risk. Your Pop, as you call him, is my aid, my companion. We have been at your side always offering protection. We were instructed on how to give you protection and guidance. Yes, we have ability, but we used our ability to sense the correct time to act. This does not need the same talent that you have." With a lighter note she added, "The punch to the head was a first I must say, quite entertaining in fact." Ash's great-grandfather simply nodded.

"Ash, this is not the end of matters for you. The future is uncertain, you must remain focused as you will be needed somewhere at some time in the future. It is not clear when or where, but a time will come when you will need all at your disposal. Your talent has not been tested fully yet. It was the love for your family that sent that filthy demon Lord back to hell, but you will be asked to do more. We will not be able to assist you in the future, our task is complete. Ash we love you, your mother loves you, but she is unaware of any of this. That is the way it must be. Oh, by the way, Happy Birthday, that fact was of no matter."

Ash asked, "What has become of Brian?" She replied with a heavy heart, "Brian opened up his inner-being to those who would lie to him and harm him. His hunger for power and wealth lead him down a path that many travel, but sadly Brian crossed the line, and once crossed there is no return. His actions were influenced by the demon Lord. It was not quite chance that the both of you met and spent so much time together. As I said, a demon Lord is a powerful enemy, however it needed the means to enter this realm. Brian gave him that means; Brian sold his soul. Only at the end did he fully realise what he had done. He will stay in purgatory forever."

As Ash carefully listened to the detail being laid out by his gran he was also aware that embedded within this information was more knowledge which was essential for him to receive. This information was stored within the newly activated part of his mind, it would be acted on later.

All three stood close together, it was strange Ash thought, that they had been chatting for what seemed like hours, but in fact had only been twenty minutes. It was clear that all that needed to be said was said. Ash's grandmother placed her hand against his cheek and said, "It is time to leave now, come along old Pop we are done."

Both his grandmother and Pop became transparent. She put out her hand and stroked the side of his face once more; his great grandfather did the same. As well as information being transferred so were the essences of the profound love they shared. Ash said, "Rest well, Gran, Pop, we will be together in another time, know that I love you very dearly." Both Gran and Pop slowly blended into the beautiful view. Both smiled at Ash then were gone.

Chapter 17
Ash's Mother

Twelve months later, Ash, who had continued his job, and continued to investigate and learn from the knowledge he had been given, had made more than regular contact with his family. On one occasion he took his visiting mother for a drive into the mountains. Ash said, "You rarely talk about my Grandmother." This was a subject that Ash's mother struggled to address. Ash said, "She died when I was very young. I do not have any real memories of her, what was she like?" Ash's mother replied in a quiet voice: "Your gran loved you very much. She wanted to spend every moment with you, she would care for you when I had to go to work, she was never as happy as when she was with you. Your gran was a tough lady. She might have been small, but she was acute and as sharp as a pin. Her silver-grey hair sometimes looked as if it were glowing," then Ash's mother went quiet. Ash knew that the next part was difficult for her but he needed his mother to let go of this memory which she had carried for almost thirty years. Ash said, "Yes go on, you have my full attention." His mother gathered herself and continued: "One day your gran turned up and said to me, why don't you take yourself to the shops dear, buy something nice for yourself. Well, I was ready for a break, you were such an easy child to care for and I had complete trust in Mum, so I agreed and left. Oh, how I wish I had stayed, but your gran insisted I go and enjoy myself. When I returned, the house was so quiet and still, nothing moved. I called, there was no reply." His mother began to quietly weep. Ash said very tenderly, "Go on Mum, what happened next?"

Bracing herself, Ash's mother continued: "I walked into the sitting room. Everything seemed in order, however above the fireplace in the wall was a small crack, I could not recall that previously. There was black stuff dripping from the crack. I thought, oh these old coal fires, then thought no more about it. I then went into the parlor. This is where you would play for hours. Mother's favourite chair was in the corner; you were fast asleep in her arms. I thought Mother was sleeping. I touched her on the shoulder, and knew immediately. They say she died in her sleep, she had a weakness in her heart and simply fell to sleep holding her beloved Grandson."

There was a brief silence. Ash extended his hand to his mother. She took it and held it to her face.

"Oh, Ash, I should never have left her with you, I should have been there." Quietly crying his mother let go of this bitter memory. She had told Ash something she could never talk about previously, Ash absorbed this memory without his mother knowing, she was now free of this painful thought. Quite suddenly his mother turned to Ash and said, "The strange thing is that over the years when I thought about Mum, I swear I could smell the scent of Daphne. This was your gran's favourite shrub, she loved the scent." Ash said nothing, he smiled to himself.

They arrived at his gran's resting place, a small cemetery under the shadow of the mountains.

"I am not sure why my mother wanted to be put to rest here, but it is so peaceful don't you think?"

Laying fresh flowers on the grave, Ash said quietly, "I love you Gran, say hello to Pop."

Later that evening, while not thinking of anything in

particular, a headache arrived and his teeth began to hurt. Within Ash an automatic pulse of energy released, its target was the demon attempting to violate him. This demon was no match for Ash's abilities and it was expelled efficiently and swiftly. However, when he looked more closely at the demon, he recognised more detail and with a heavy heart said, "Brian."

ASH

Chapter 1
Ash

To suggest that his life was less dramatic would be misleading. Ash was equipped with the knowledge that he had received from his grandmother and great grandfather. During the day, his work took him into the homes of people with needs. Using his occupational skills, Ash was mostly able to create a plan for the individual or individuals and their families to follow which would to some extent relieve the situation.

In one instance, Ash was tasked to visit a home where it had been reported that the young children were being abused, not in a sexual way, but more in a bullying way. The family in question lived in a large detached house. The father was a successful small business owner, the children wanted for very little, but sadly the mother called Jane suffered from self-confidence issues. This lead her to drink, which she was able to hide from most people but sadly her children who she loved would suffer when her needs depended on the contents of a wine bottle. Of course, she was in complete denial about the amount she consumed, hiding bottles in places around the home.

The two children who were six and eight knew when the bullying was about to begin, usually when their father was away for short periods on business, the children would hide together in their bedrooms, frightened that their mother would rant and rage at them — seeing their mother change from the usual caring mum into the scary vindictive termagant. They would only rest when the mother fell into an alcohol-induced sleep. Nothing was said when the sober mother continued her life in a hazy sluggish manner the next morning.

The case came about as a result of a chance comment to a school teacher by the youngest child. Calls were made, and Ash was asked to look at the case.

Ash arrived at the home at about eleven in the morning. He was greeted by the youngest child, who announced, "Mummy, we have a visitor."

"Yes, show whoever it is into the sitting room. I will be down shortly," answered the mother in a heavy tone. Ash was taken by a little hand into the sitting room. During this brief encounter with the child, Ash was able to see quite clearly the issues, love, fear and confusion. Touching the small hands, Ash found the area within the child's soul where he was able to instill a sense of comfort and reassurance. Of course, the child knew no better at the time but would very soon feel much happier and confident about matters and of course, his mummy.

Ash looked around the sitting room, searching for any other clues as to why there were issues in this family. He saw on a small side table a grouping of silver picture frames. One of the frames was face down. Ash picked this frame up and saw images of two older people frozen in time on the photograph. They looked very happy together. Ash closed his eyes and searched for answers, quickly he knew that this was an image of this mother's beloved parents, they had both died suddenly only a year or so earlier, and the shock of their early departure had never gone away. Ash returned the picture frame to the table and stood it up.

After a couple of minutes, a pale-faced young woman walked into the sitting room. She wore casual clothes, and they had clearly been slept in. Ash sensed her heavy heart and also the effects of her binge drinking which lead to this particular hangover. He said nothing, just waited.

Ash then introduced himself: "Hi, my name is Ash. I am here as a friend, there is nothing for you or your family to worry about, why don't you take a seat next to the children." Buried in these words was a calming and reassuring message which Ash placed in her mind. She looked at Ash through glazed foggy eyes and sat in between both children. They both instinctively snuggled into their mother's side getting into the most comfortable position they could.

Ash sat in a comfortable chair opposite the three. He casually waved a hand, the ticking of the clock on the mantle shelf began to slow; the air in the room warmed slightly and a wonderful smell of home baking filled the room. Ash felt Jane's heartbeat slow down. He also heard the deep breathing of the children who were now cuddled up to their mother safely and soundly asleep. Ash had subtly calmed the tension in the house and made the children sleep, and while they slept, he purged them of any hurtful thoughts and memories.

Ash said, "Jane, it was not your fault that you were unable to arrive home before your father passed away, or that, broken-hearted and soon after your mother joined him. You must understand that they both loved you and your family and still do. They are together and very happy. The time has now come when you will no longer need to fight with this matter. You can continue with your lives, pick up a time before your heartache without the need to hide and hurt yourself." Jane, too, was sleeping on the sofa with her children, but she acknowledged what Ash had said. The colour in her face changed. Her complexion was now fresh and healthy.

It was a simple enough process, mind-mending, and Ash had become proficient. This, of course as a result of the in-depth teachings from his grandmother. A little like editing a home movie, replaying the contents, once that was done the information could be transferred to the mixing suite where by fast forwarding, rewinding, adding other memories and deleting unwelcome ones and finally mastering the film and sound track all was put into sense and emotional order. The fixed movie could then be returned to the individual without them knowing.

Ash stood up and said, "Well, that is that then, I will see myself out, goodbye." Ash left the family in the house.

A short time later that day, Jane woke up with both children. She hugged each of them and said, "I think we will visit your gran and granddad's grave. It is about time we took more flowers for them, I do miss them both, but I am sure that they are happy together in that special place." The children agreed, and all three gathered wildflowers and left for the churchyard. During the short journey, there was no mention of the visit from Ash. In fact none of them had any memories of previous issues or worries at all. They simply enjoyed the family love that they all shared.

The file with the report about the family vanished, and memories of all concerned left the front of mind forever.

Chapter 2
The Croft

Ash continued to work in an almost invisible way. Being able to cover his tracks, he could remove bad memories and heal deep emotional wounds. Of course, there were occasions where Ash could not influence matters. Sometimes he was simply there to offer comfort, particularly towards the end of life for the elderly and in some cases young sick people. Ash was able to slip in and out of the hospital wards as well as the hospices and all other places to assist. No memory of his visits were recalled, the only less than lucid comments would come from those he had visited. On occasions, some of those who were about to pass on would say, "Oh! but he was such a lovely boy." The visiting families sitting around the bed would look at each other and say, for example, "Who was?" and with a smile, the families would receive a casual reply," Yes, that lovely young man, he visits me you know."

Family members would again look at each other, but they too would receive a little comfort knowing that just before the passing of their loved ones, they would say, "Well, at least she was in a happy place and with no pain."

As time passed, Ash received more instruction from his grandmother. He placed himself into a trance. In this state, he was able to cross over to another realm, a safe hidden place where time had little influence, although time never stands still. If this was to happen, all of creation would be undone.

He loved the time spent with his gran, she was a

formidable woman. Ash was aware that the instructions being given by his gran were derived from somewhere else, a somewhere that sat just far enough out of reach of his mind but there all the same.

"Reach deeper, fold your mind voice, command and unleash your will," his gran said with a firm tone. She smiled as Ash concentrated his force of will onto a practice demon. The demon shrieked and, in a flash of crimson light, vanished.

'Practice demons' are demons who have been expelled from the earthly realm and held in suspension until needed for training purposes. It seems that there is a never-ending supply of these entities attempting to defile the human race.

And so Ash's instruction continued, his ability to become more invisible to others strengthened, and he was able to move around people and places more freely as well as unseen. On occasion, an individual may say, "Did you see that?" "See what?" came the response. "You're seeing things. No, I thought! Oh, never mind, it's not important."

The time came when his gran told Ash that it was essential for him to leave his normal job and to relocate to a more remote location. A time of importance was approaching quickly, and he was required.

And so Ash relocated to a small croft house. Driving down a long uneven track through the most beautiful Highland landscape he passed a great emperor stag. Ash stopped his car and wound down the car window. The stag remained still as it gazed at Ash. Its gaze penetrated his eyes, and the words 'welcome' followed. The stag turned and casually trotted away.

The track was long, and Ash was aware that he was passing through fields of pure energy almost like driving through a mirage. He arrived at his new white-washed home. It had two small windows to the front, a red tin roof, and a tall chimney. A rich ultramarine blue front door welcomed its visitor. This was a place of safety.

To further stay out of sight and more to the point, out of mind, prior to Ash leaving, he had to discretely place information and thoughts into the minds of his closest family. They would not think about Ash, and if they did, the thought melted away from the front of mind. Ash was safe, and so were his nearest and dearest.

The one person who would be more difficult to deal with was his mother. And so it was necessary for him to visit her and place protective barriers around her, and so with great care and skill while sitting and chatting over a cuppa he was able to place into his mother's mind that Ash was safe, well, fine and happy, any time he popped into her mind, the inserted simple thought would come to the forefront of her mind, and she could get on with her life quite contented and happy. Ash was also content that he had given his mother protection from any danger she may encounter. While he gently probed his mother's mind he sensed something that he was familiar with but could not bring to the front of his mind. As quickly as the feeling came, so it evaporated, he thought no more about it.

The Croft was exceptionally comfortable with a warm atmosphere of love and caring. He and his grandmother covered many more subjects.

Quite suddenly on a bright and sunny morning, while taking a bowl of porridge his gran had made, she said, "Ash, my dear, dear boy, the time has come for me to leave, I can not teach you anymore, but you have so much more to learn. You are special, more than you know and I will always be at your side, be careful. I will keep an eye on your mother too." With that, his grandmother opened the front door and stepped outside, where she vanished.

Chapter 3
The Visitor

Ash continued to practice what he had learned. He was becoming more aware that he would be tested, that an attack could happen at any time. Events were taking place. He sensed a battle was coming, and he was going to be part of the fight between what he stood for and powerful evil intentions. The need to concentrate on learning his skills became more and more urgent.

The wind whispered and whistled outside, rain carried by the wind gently played rhythmic sounds on the red tin roof. Ash was concentrating on how to read the intentions within demon mind. This was not so difficult because a demon only has one thought, and that is to cause chaos. His concentration was so intense that when a loud knock on the door came, he immediately, without a thought, armed himself, he was alert and ready, pulsing with charged energy. 'Excellent, yes, excellent!' A clear voice spoke in his mind. There was no need to respond as Ash had known about this voice for some time now.

Ash pushed his mind to the door and instantly was aware that whoever was on the other side of the door was talented, to what extent or on which side he could not determine. Then, bang! as if a gust of wind hit the door, it sprang open.

Standing quite still with hands on hips on the door threshold was a small plump man. He had a hairstyle that reminded Ash of Friar Tuck. The man's red face was serious and gave no hint as to his age, his clothing appeared to be a collection of plain clean rags sewn together randomly, and he had no shoes. His feet were bare but clean. Behind this man was a bright light which weakened very quickly and disappeared. The man said, "Well aren't you going to invite me in then, it's freezing out here, and I'm soaked to the wings." Ash found this amusing and, with a slight grin, said, "Oh, yes, please, please come in out of the weather." The strange little man crossed the threshold and entered the croft.

Immediately Ash knew who this man was. He said, "You are my tutor; welcome to my home." Ash then respectfully nodded his head, and all his defences were lowered. In an instant Ash felt a thump in his torso. He flew across the room and landed softly against the floor. 'Never, never let your defences down before you are sure with whom you are engaging with. I thought you had taught him better.' The question was not aimed at Ash, 'over to you now my dear.' It was the voice of his gran, Ash acknowledging with a head nod and a smile touched his lips; he then met the eyes of his new tutor and once again gave a deeper respectful nod of his head. "Oh, enough of that, a cup of hot water would be very welcome, however."

Ash fetched a mug of hot water from the constantly filled kettle that was constantly bubbling away on the stove and handed the steaming beverage to his visitor and said, "What a surprise after all of this time." His guest said nothing but looked around the interior of the small kitchen with its table, the two windows, and thick walls. His guest smiled to himself and said, "Yes, what a surprise."

Ash sat at the table opposite his new tutor. Steam was escaping from the hot water in the cup; then Ash became aware that time was slowing. He did not know why but he knew who was responsible as he could feel his guest silently working, slower and slower, it seemed that the clock on the mantle had stopped completely. Ash was aware that time within his home was different to the outer world, but this time was even slower. His guest said, "Good, very good, at least you have learned that. Identifying the subtlest changes in time is difficult; you have done well." His guest continued in a serious tone: "Ash, I rarely enter this realm in human form; however, matters are upon us, and we must act. You are a talented man, your grandmother has seen to that, you have applied your gifts to those who were in need, you have offered compassion and love where required, and you have taken on my instructions very well. Oh, yes, it was I who instructed your gran in the first place and your great grandfather too. I have been tending to your family line it seems forever. The tasks you have engaged in have been preparing you for matters that will affect the whole of mankind and planet Earth. Ash, there is a war raging, a war that began before this universe came into being.

This planet, together with a couple of other similar planets, out of all of the other bodies within the universes are special, Earth being the most special and also the most prized and desired."

The opening statement from his guest took Ash by surprise. He was aware that a war was taking place, but something on this scale was almost unbelievable. Ash said, "But what can I do about it? I cannot save the planet!"

His visitor said, "That is quite true, Ash, there is not one single entity that can save the destiny of the planet, it requires so much more, but your role is more important than others. You have shown that you have great ability. Your encounter with the demon Lord proved that, but where you go from here will require much more than you know. That is why I am here now, Ash. Even though we can slow time, we cannot stop time, and matters are unfolding even as we speak. You are not the only one with a gift.

Balance requires that equality must be maintained; however those who we do battle with have other ideas. They do not acknowledge balance in the same way as we must.

There are many others who were born with a gift. Some simply never realised it. They were targeted by those who coveted what the other possessed, and sadly they are no longer on this plain. Others, realising that they were different, used their gifts openly, showed off, squandered the results, and in time will lose all, so many will lose their souls. You understand that aspect Ash, as well as Brian ultimately did."

Ash said, "You know about Brian?" As soon as Ash spoke the words, he knew it was a foolish question. There was no reply. There was no need to.

His instructor continued, "There are those who have the gift and received further instruction. They do battle in regions around the globe. As I have said, Ash, we are in the midst of a war, a war that we believed had been averted. Back in the history of the planet, a battle was fought. The result was peace and balance. However, what we did not realise was that a destructive Seed had remained. This Seed has grown once again. It is strong and has influenced many. It has converted tens of thousands, you see Ash, the Seed is the offspring of my brother Greed."

With a heavy, sad sigh, the visitor continued, "The desire to 'have' for have's sake has grown. Like I have stated, there will be Balance, and so where we have someone with your ability, so there will be another spawned from the Seed of Greed with an equal talent. Sadly the Seed has spread. Its purpose once again is to have the Earth for itself. It does not acknowledge Balance, it is blind to all other than itself. So Ash it is not your task to save this beautiful world, no no, we must work together and once and for all rid this planet of the vile and unholy essence of the Seed of Greed".

Quietly absorbing these words , the enormity of what Ash had just heard began to overwhelm his senses. He was being physically and emotionally crushed by the weight of the reality of the situation. He looked at his guest; tears fell from Ash's eyes. His guest smiled at Ash.

As his guest smiled, pure inner strength ignited within Ash, an explosion of pure energy pulsed through his body and soul, clarity and understanding replaced the clouds that had up to this point hidden the real situation, he pushed the weight that was crushing him away, then Ash understood, this had been a test, a test to see if he was capable of understanding the dire situation he, they and the world was in. He also realised that he had always had this knowledge, but until this moment, it had been carefully shielded from him because up until this moment, he would not have been able to assimilate its weight. It was not the right time. But now he understood. He was prepared.

His guest stood up and said, "You are ready for your next instruction Ash. Your understanding of the enormous amount of information you have just received will prepare you for your next test. His tutor's voice softened and said, "Ash the next test will be the most painful test of all!"

Ash stood up. He noticed that the steam was still raising from his guest's mug; however the date on the timepiece on the mantle shelf showed that two days had passed since his tutor had arrived and they had both sat at the table for all of this time. Somehow his tutor had installed in Ash's mind the Earth's history up to this date. Ash wondered what could be more painful than what he had just heard. Ash turned to his tutor and said, "Who are you?" The reply came in a matter-of-fact tone.

"Ash, I am Compassion and Love, in another time I was Peter." With a sharp intake of breath, but not surprised, Ash said, "Of course it was you who fought Greed. I feel your pain." This knowledge too was exposed only seconds ago. That last comment raised his tutor's eyebrow! Ash said, "May I call you Peter?"

"Why yes, that would be quite acceptable."

"We must leave soon, Ash, you must also be aware that since taking residence in this house, more time has passed than you have been aware of. Your home was once a place I called my 'special safe place', a place that when I needed to, I could visit and be completely safe and invisible from almost everything outside of here, but you already know that?" Peter said, raising an eyebrow again.

"Yes, I suppose I do," Ash replied. Peter continued, "What you are not aware of is that you are a target, you have always been a target; however you have been shielded to greater extents, the true nature of your inner-self has been hidden from almost every entity in the universes until now including yourself, and so, for the time we have been together you have been searched for by those who wish to kill and destroy you, and I mean destroy, to wipe you out of all that there is and will ever be, they will stop at nothing to prevent you from achieving your full potential. The search for you has crossed many lines, balance has not been observed and innocent people have perished as a result." Peter's tone became softer and compassionate, "Ash, unrelenting energy has been spent on the search for you. You have been quite safe here, but each time you ventured out you gave hints of your location. Ash, the other side has located your mother's home, they have taken her too. Your mother has been hurt beyond human suffering at the will of one of the most feared of all demons. The demon calls itself Raths; he is a general in hell's army. He has been searching for you for many many years and now he is attempting to force your location from your mother. You have done well to protect your mother from harm, but I have to tell you that her soul is in danger, and she may not survive her ordeal."

Chapter 4
Ash's Mother

Patricia Isobel Lewis was a plain and simple girl, simple in her appearance but not her mind. She was sharp and very capable just like her mother. Fashion and makeup meant little to her, in fact, there was no need to cover her beautiful fresh features. An athletic young lady full of life itself and a caring person who put others before herself, she had a close relationship with her mother, who lived close by. Although she had many caring and friendly associates, she never had a boyfriend. She was content and simply got on with living. This was to change on a warm summer's night.

Pat walked carefree through a local forest soaking up the dappled light and warmth as the sun softly beamed its light through the trees, birdsong filled her heart with joy, a deer ahead stood quite still its deep brown eyes reflected a shaft of light, winking at her as it sprang out of sight into the deep emerald trees. The air was cool and fresh. Pat felt more alive than she had ever felt. She had an affinity with nature, she could sense life within the trees, she even thought she could hear them chattering together.

She sat below a large silver birch tree, her back supported by the strong silvery copper trunk. She tilted her head backwards slightly and looked up at the overhanging branches which were laden with translucent lime coloured leaves, the sunlight and leaves shimmered and blended together, a long shaft of light found its way through the abundance of leaves, it touched her face, and she felt as though a soft finger had stroked her cheek, the touch was so tender it made her blush. She unwrapped her packed lunch, sandwich spread, and ham on fresh bread with cheese and onion crisps followed by homemade elderflower cordial. Pat was in her heaven. Relaxed and content, she closed her eyes. In her mind's eye were lights of all colours dancing to a tune that was just audible, the leaves singing in hushed tones in her mind, a harp and violin strings played as one, the sound accompanied the chorus of gentle birdsong, she did not think about the sound, she accepted it for what it was, soothing and comforting, soon Pat was in a deep and peaceful sleep.

A leaf detached from a branch high above Pat's head, it floated softly downwards each tilt caught the sunlight and reflected downward, the tiny shafts of light touched her serine face, and she began to return from her slumber, the small translucent leaf landed on her opened hand in her lap, even as it settled on her palm, the leaf shimmered and blended into her skin where it vanished.

Pat woke up. She had no concept of the time. In the sky, the sun had clearly moved, a question about how long she had been under the tree faded away. It was not important. What was important was that she felt energised and refreshed; then another question entered into her mind, she asked herself, 'What is different?', as she reached for her drink and swallowed the sweet flowery beverage, all thoughts and questions evaporated with her thirst. Pat simply knew she was safe and happy.

She stood up and stretched before heading back through the woods. During her return, she felt that she was being followed. She stopped and looked around. There was nothing. She dismissed the sensation. She once again felt comforted. She was not alone. Skipping and singing to herself, she returned home in what seemed no time, as if time itself had slowed down! Pat swept her hair back with her hand, the hand that had somehow absorbed the leaf. At the touch of her hand against her head, she felt a tingling feeling. It was good to be alive. She continued home. Her mother arrived shortly afterwards, as she greeted her daughter, a rich smile covered her face, she embraced her daughter and and in her mind whispered "Welcome to my grandson within you."

Not one question was asked. It was as if nothing was different. Her friends came and went leaving her in peace. Pat gave no thought to her situation; there was nothing to think about. She was safe, and in fantastic health. All of her needs were attended to by her mother. What was there to be concerned about? The child she carried was normal, and all was good. The birth of Ash occurred quietly, and without a fuss, Of course Pats's mother was in attendance and of course Pat gave no thought to the gentle midwife who visited her and was there for the birth. "Everything is as it should be dear," the tiny lady would whisper to her, then with a soft brush of her finger across Pat's cheek she said, "It is time for me to leave now; you are in safe hands," indicating her mother who sat quite patiently in the room. Both the midwife and Pat's mother seemed to know each other, or had Pat just thought it appeared that way. The midwife stood and said, "You and Ash are special to me, I will watch over you both." When the midwife left, Pat thought, 'Ash, yes, how wonderful, you are Ash.' The infant gazed into his mother's eyes. The bond was complete. Pat's mother said to her inner mind, "it is done". Unaware to Pat, the forest from where the leaf had derived burst into tree song, together with the birds, the sounds could be heard for many miles around.

Chapter 5
Prepared

Peter could sense the anger and pain that coursed through Ash. He felt the immediate intentions he was forming within him. He felt the power pulsing with each heavy heartbreaking breath that Ash inhaled and explosively exhaled, a power which out of control would be devastating for himself and the planet.

With calm but firm instruction, Peter said, "No, Ash, you must not act in that way; it would be disastrous, you have an opportunity to rescue your mother, but you and her will be in great peril." Ash snapped angrily, "Can't you help, can't you stop this demon?" Tears flowed down Ash's face. "How could you let this happen?" He demanded, "How?"

Peter replied, "Ash, know that I have always protected Pat, your mother. I have given her inner- comfort and strength, even though she is being humiliated and hurt. She will feel my presence she always has; that is my gift to her. It is up to you to do the rest, for if I interfere at this point, our enemy will know our intentions and great damage will have been done. All that I have put into place will be put in peril. No, Ash, this is your task alone. I have great faith in you. Now we must leave; time has picked up the pace once more."

Ash controlled his emotions, he looked into the face of Peter and he said, "I am ready, I am grateful for your personal visit. I understand how much this has meant to you; thank you, oh by the way," Ash added now he was back in control, "you made a wonderful midwife."

A rich and warm smile touched Peter's face, "Why, thank you," Peter said, then continued, "I will take you by other means to within easy travelling distance of where you need to be. You will know the location of where you are going and know what you must do. This will be the last time we meet in this realm Ash. I have faith in you, my son." Peter opened his arms, and where rags had been now, there were beautiful translucent wings. Pulsating with pure energy. The wings were enormous. They gathered Ash within their reach surrounding both Ash and Peter. In a blaze of incandescent light they were no longer in the croft. Ash could see details far below him, mountains, loch's, bright city lights, then travelling at such high speed details below blurred.

Within what seemed like seconds, Ash felt earth under his feet. The light that had surrounded him absorbed into his soul. Ash felt the purity of its power invigorating him. A quick scan informed Ash that he was in central London, his task was about to unfold, and there was no time to be spared. Peter had vanished but left words in the mind of Ash, 'caution now, caution.'

Chapter 6
Lord Raths

Deep in their lair, the battalion of demons led by Lord Raths frantically went about their individual and unit tasks. There were two subjects that dominated. The first was the imminent arrival of the ultimate Master, son of Greed and the many attempts to capture the 'bastard human, Ash'. One without the other created so much tension within the hive that tempers which were always on a short leash flared, many underlying demons and novices were destroyed or simply left to further rot in a darker slime infested corner. The slime of course, slowly but surely and painfully consumed the residual life remaining in the victim until nothing was left.

Lord Raths summoned several of his lieutenants,

"What news on that human Ash, when will I have him, soon maybe, perhaps," he snapped, this was neither a question more of a demand, his tone was cold and harsh, he cast his flaring tiny red piggy like eyes over his gathered subordinates and stopped, looking directly at a newly promoted minor demon who flinched in terror at the sudden gaze, "You!, what progress? I hope for your sake it pleases me."

The minor demon trembled on the spot, pustules surrounding its hollow eyes oozed, thick hot fluid fell onto the slimy wet dank ground, a shaking gnarled claw wiped the discharge away, its face visibly paled in colour and his eyes looked down onto the ground, "He evaded us my Lord," he stated in a low guttural tone. *CRACK!* The sound of a whip filled the space, the demon Lord's face contorted with anger as he thrust his gnarled boney hand toward his minion, a fiery spindle of intense red energy left the Lord's outstretched arm it and wrapped itself around the soldier. The demon Lord Raths roared, "This is the price of failure. Find him!" Instantaneously the thread of pure red hatred tightened around the soldier and sliced him in two; then both halves of his body exploded, the remains shimmered and bled into the already present black slime mass which accepted the victim readily.

Chapter 7
Goodge Street Underground

The moonlit night revealed where Ash was located. He was in Tottenham Court Road. In Central London the silhouetted Post Office Tower loomed high above his head; its shadow seemed to go for miles.

The street was quiet. Only yellow flashing lights of the council vehicles could be seen reflecting off the glazed windows of shops and offices. Ash was standing opposite the entrance to Gooch Street underground tube station. This station has one of the deepest access shafts within the tube system and one of the oldest rickety lifts. Ash was immediately aware that this is where he must go. He could detect the vile smell of sulphur and decay escaping from this hole in the ground. More to the point, he could feel the presence of his mother, she was deep underground somewhere and she was suffering.

Ash entered the deep stair shaft. He had adjusted his physical state: he appeared like a mirage. He shimmered and blended into whatever backdrop was available, all but invisible. Stealthily, he began his descent. The air that rose from the depths of the shaft was sickly and warm, made worse by the putrid odour that accompanied it. There was another familiar nasty smell present, and that was rotting eggs, evil's signature, sulphur. The presence of this alerted Ash to the presence of serious opposition. He was entering the spider's web. Here he felt the essence of formidable demons. He continued down. During the training in his Highland home, Ash was instructed in many and varied methods on how to protect himself and others when confronted with an adversary who posed a real threat. Simulations were created where Ash could practice and fine-tune his abilities. He was also shown the variety of demons and other entities that he might encounter, from the lowest hell army rank to the generals who lead the legions. Ash was instructed on how to recognise when demons possessed innocent human individuals and how to identify demons who occupy other forms. This was more difficult to identify because the higher the rank, the more ability to deceive, a possessed individual might appear quite normal but all the time is a possession by a demon.

A swift and simple thought would disarm an attacking entity. Focusing and pinpointing his will, Ash was able to return to hell or the holding realm of minor demons. This he could do without informing any others of his presence. Ash also shared one other ability when he needed it: the 'special and safe place' was always there and available to escape to instantly. In that place, he was completely safe and hidden from all view.

In the dimly-lit stairwell, Ash continued to descend. Reaching the tube station level, he now searched for the entrance from where the sulphurous odour was escaping.

At the base of the stairs just out of sight and not detectable by most others, Ash found what he was looking for.

The doorway was made up of the same black and white tiles as the stairwell and blended perfectly into the grouting. It was seamless. Ash placed his hand onto the door; it opened with a quiet swish. Ash stepped through; the door silently closed behind him. When the door was again secure, Ash walked a few paces forward. He could see quite well as the space he was in was lit by a dull green light. The smell of sulphur was strong, and the temperature became much higher. Charged air particles shimmered all around him.

Ash found another stairwell; he began to walk silently down. He could not tell how far below ground he was but as he descended, the walls surrounding the stairs became rock. On the rock, green-black slime slowly dripped. The slime was just alive. It knew Ash and quivered in agitation. He knew he was getting closer and that there was great danger ahead in this place.

Ash arrived at what appeared to be the bottom of the dank, dark hellhole. Every part of his body was alert; he could sense others in the large space in front of him. Ash could see details through the dimness. To his left, he saw what looked like a series of rotted wooden doors. Ash could hear moans and groans coming from whatever or whoever was behind the doors. To his right was another series of doors. These were all intact; they seemed to be shimmering, alive, dangerous. Straight ahead several hundred meters or so was a temple. It had been fashioned out of the rock face; it too was dripping with black slime accompanied by a faint deep yellow, luminous green glow. In front of the temple was an altar. Within the temple glowed dark flames, almost purple-black, and there was movement.

Chapter 8
The Prisoners

He moved forward more slowly, Ash went to the first rotting door. He felt his way using only his mind, the room or cell was occupied, and it was not a demon. He entered the rancid cell space, and a surge of revulsion came as Ash saw laying on the cold damp, filthy floor a young man. The man covered his head with bloodied, trembling hands, he was whimpering. Deep fresh flesh wounds covered his back, warm blood slowly seeped from the lacerations. The soles of his feet were blackened and burned; it was clear the poor man had been tortured. Ash knelt down next to him and touched his filthy, bloodied hand. The man flinched in terror. Ash quickly and silently soothed the man's pain, both physically and mentally. A few more thoughts and where burned feet were, now healing was rapidly taking place. Ash whispered, "You are safe. I am a friend. How did you get here?"

The young man turned his face to Ash and said in a shivering, weak voice, "I was with friends, we were invited to a party, when we arrived we were given drinks, then I woke up here. Where am I? I've been here so long now! They hurt me; they are monsters" Ash could see that the young man had several days of beard growth on his face, and he was dehydrated. He also saw the terrible mark on the man's temple. An attempt had been made to remove his soul but had failed. Ash concentrated a while holding the young man's hand, he looked into his memories; he discovered that he had been out with his friends. They had been drinking when they were approached by a smartly- dressed woman. Ash knew that she was, in fact, a demon foot soldier.

The demon told the group of young people about a party a few streets away, and they were invited. When they arrived at the mid-terrace townhouse, they were all given a glass of champagne. Immediately after they drank the liquor, they fell unconscious. However, this young man's mind recalled the demon saying, "The Master will be pleased with us. This lot will give him more pure souls." His memory then went blank.

Ash placed 'hope' and an escape plan into the front of the young victim's mind, then put him in a deep comfortable sleep until the time for escape was ready. By now, Ash knew that there were nine more pitiful victims in a similar condition. Quickly and confidently, but most importantly, with silence, Ash repaired terrible bodily injuries and gave instructions to the other poor victims. His plan was ready.

Ash stood quite still, the will of energy inside of him focused, he sent out one thought to the young people, the escape went into action. Each victim came to, each felt refreshed and ready to run, a second thought reached out. Quietly all ten young people opened their filthy cell doors, and one by one, quickly and quietly made their way to the stairwell. Once there, each person sprinted faster than they had ever moved in their lives. They ran without effort. They climbed up the spiral stairwell until they emerged intoTottenham Court Road, where they ran in different directions—they were now safe.

Chapter 9
Sacrifice

O nce Ash was aware that they were safe, he left the last cell. Without warning, a door opened opposite him. A smartly-dressed woman came out of the door. It was the same woman Ash had seen in the victims minds, she had seduced her young victims. She turned towards the inner-sanctum, unaware of the great escape. She was no threat to Ash, and so he followed her. She was not aware that he was following.

Then the woman demon said to another who joined her, "The woman still gives nothing away about her bastard son! She is able to withstand all of my attempts to get into her mind; he must have taken steps to protect her." The other demon at her side said, "Our Master will arrive soon, then he will open her mind and take what he wants. Her son's will shall be broken into pieces at our Master's word." This information gave Ash hope of rescuing his mother; it was clear that the demon general had not yet arrived. However, Ash could not sense where his mother's location was; clearly, she was being shielded. After all, they wanted him, not his mother. He followed the two demons deeper into the temple space. All of a sudden, there was a loud terrifying scream. Turning around to locate the source of the distress, Ash saw a young girl being dragged from inside of the temple building by two none demons. She was taken toward the altar. A small procession of people followed the screaming girl; several of the hideous followers mocked the girl's terror.

Ash knew that the followers were not demons—they

were part of the growing army of humans who were prepared to give their souls to satisfy their own desires. They were doomed, of course. Ash could see that all of these men and women were in their normal day clothes: several men in suits and ties, probably a senior banker, power-dressed women, and others, but what offended Ash most was in the middle of this unholy rank was a priest. He was walking next to a recognisable politician; she had a grim look on her face, and they chatted to one another quite casually.

The girl was lifted above their heads even though she was wriggling violently, her scream filling the air; several of the group then placed her onto and held her down on the altar. The girl continued to thrash and scream wildly. Ash felt her terror.

SMASH! A heavy blow to the side of her head, the girl fell silent. Fresh blood trickled from an open wound on the side of her face. Unconscious she was tied to the altar with what appeared to be heavy rope. It was not rope but black sticky strands; her clothing was torn from her body revealing white skin. On closer examination, Ash could see deep raw bloody red and black marks on the girl's body where she had been tortured. The victim moaned.

Silence filled the vile space as the two demons Ash had been following took their position at the altar. The woman demon said in a matter-of-fact way, "Your next task will be to kill this girl and drink her blood. That will take you closer to what you desire. Oh yes, you will drink her blood from the skin that each of you will peel from her when she wakes up. The aroma of fear in the blood is so refreshing."

The woman demon looked at the gathered group and said in a rasping tone, "Do you all understand?" Ash could hear a couple of sharp intakes of air from the group and one smartly-dressed young man said in a quiet voice, "But I thought we were only going to frighten them, not carve them up, alive, and drink their blood!, The young man retched, his face contorted in horror, hot white foam escaped from between his quivering lips.

The woman demon approached the young man. Hatred ran through her body as she said to him, "Weak young fool, did you think that your desires were going to come so cheaply? *DID YOU?*" She screamed at him, "You can make the first cut, and I will be right behind you!"

The young man backed away. Trembling and weeping, he said, "I can't do it. I didn't think it was going to be like this. I can't do it!" The woman demon calmly said, "That is fine," and instantly she lifted him up by his neck, he gargled a scream, his eyes bulged out of their sockets, and his feet which of course were no longer touching the ground, thrashed about, hot urine stained his denim jeans, his lips swollen and purple burst open, blood covered his pointed chin, several of the watching group recoiled and turned their heads away. "Watch and understand," she hissed at the group, "You have made your choices. *NOW*, see what happens if you change your *MIND!*" Her other hand took hold of the young man's head, her fingers lengthened and transformed into tendril-like claws. In front of the others, she pushed the fine tendrils deep into the young man's temples, penetrating the inside of his skull. The man weakly took hold of his executioner's limbs. He wriggled in her vice-like grip and swung back and forth in an attempt to free himself. His struggle was futile.

The demon was now inside his head, and she tore out a small, dimly-lit glowing globe which she popped into her mouth and swallowed. A look of exhilaration flashed across her contorted face. She dropped her limp victim. He fell to the ground, his body twitching for a while before transforming into a red-black steaming mass of slime, which melted into the floor surface and vanished. The demon looked at the others and said, in a more dangerous tone, "Anyone else wish to change their minds?" Ash knew that there was nothing he could have done to save the young man; The victim had simply walked too far down a path where there is no return. He was, however, working very quickly on a rescue plan for the young girl. Ash sensed that in the immediate area there were only these two demons. He fixed his plan in his mind.

The young girl on the altar moaned as she stirred and came too. Her eyes flashed around wide with fear, she struggled, but the binding holding her got tighter and pinned her even closer to the slab of rock. The two demons looked on as the first person, a tall, thin, almost bony woman, walked confidently to the side of the altar. Without hesitation, she took a black bladed dagger which was resting on a plinth just in front of the alter, with her other free hand forcefully grabbed the outstretched girl's left arm, the girl let out a bloodcurdling terrified scream. The woman raised the blade. As she did, her face altered; her nostrils flared, lips blackened, and her eyes flashed red, hatred fuelled her soul. She looked directly at her group and then the demons. A thin-lipped smile came as she plunged the dagger down. Together the demons said in an excited terrible tone, "Yesss, do it, your new Master demands it, *NOW!*"

A pulse of energy punched through the putrid air surrounding Ash as he revealed himself, sending several of the would-be demons flying across the slimy floor. At the same moment he focused his will, the dagger tore itself from the woman's hand, snapping several of her tightly gripping fingers. It flew across the space and embedded itself in the rock. The woman let out a loud hysterical demented scream. The force of this action sent the woman hurtling backwards, knocking over several more of the gathered crowd. Panic erupted around the altar. Several of the group picked themselves up and fled in different directions, a couple were frozen on the spot. The demons acted spontaneously: the woman demon shape-shifted into a vile rabid hyena form and attacked. The head and mouth were much wider than usual, and the black teeth dripped with thick green saliva. Her attack was short-lived as with a thought, Ash stopped her in mid-air. Frozen and motionless, he sent her howling back to hell. Ash now knew that the alarm was ringing and others would come.

The second demon recognised Ash from previous information the collective had received. In a blind terror, she ran to a closed-door, almost smashing the door open she squealed at Ash, "Any closer, and the bitch dies!" The words came out as a half confused laugh-cry.

Chapter 10
Patricia

Inside the dark room, levitating in a cocoon of green energy, was Ash's naked mother. Her eyes were half-open, exhaustion clearly visible, she had deep gaping wounds on her arms and legs and torso, and fresh blood dripped from small lacerations on her temples. She slowly looked sideways and saw her son, a tear of relief fell from her eyes.

A rage such as Ash had never felt immediately welled up within him. The sight of his tortured mother created in Ash an overwhelming desire to obliterate this place and all of its evil inhabitants. Ash also knew that he had the talent to do so. Allowing his will to gather with the intention of complete destruction of this hell, Ash became aware of another voice in his mind. It said, "No Ash, not now, save your mother and the innocent," then the voice was gone, although the words were delivered gently, they were not advising but ordering.

The demon in the doorway seemed to gloat at Ash and hissed, "She is ours, and you will never have this whore." Ash felt the demon gathering its will. It focused on Ash's mother and sent out a razor sharp shard of blackened rock. Ash responded, the missile veered sharply and impaled a stricken onlooker who was torn apart on impact. In the same instant the attacking demon's features contorted, a look of puzzled surprise flashed through its eyes, the demon stood absolutely still before vapourising, the demon was no more.

He entered the cell and quickly evaporated the shield containing his mother. She fell into his arms. He said,

"Mother, you are safe now. I will take care of you, we are leaving this place, all will be well, you brave, brave woman."

Ash cradled his mother in his arms then concentrated. As quick as a flash, he retrieved the young girl from the altar. With one more effort from Ash, they all vanished. At the same time a huge doorway opened, and an overwhelming cry of rage came from hell's gateway. The demon general Lord Raths saw Ash, and just before they vanished, the general threw its will at Ash and his mother, then they were gone.

The fabric of the interior of this evil void reverberated violently as the demon general realised that Ash had escaped. Several of the rotting doors flew off their hinges, exploding into fragments, charged particles hanging in the space spontaneously combusted. Two of the human servants were pulverised instantly. The rest of them fled in all directions. "Find him!" bellowed the general. "Bring him before me!"

Chapter 11
The Safe Place

Three people arrived instantly in the *'Safe Place'*, Ash placed his mother on one cot and the young girl the other. He knew that they were now out of harms way. He examined the extent of the torture that had been inflicted on his mother. She failed to give the details so badly required by her captors. They had failed to locate her son but at a great physical cost to herself.

Deep dark flesh wounds on her back, areas of skin that had been torn off, large blackened areas of bruising. Ash felt his heart tremble with rage, but more than that, he felt the overwhelming love he had for his mother. This quelled his anger.

She looked with exhausted eyes at Ash and in a weak voice barely audible spoke, *"Ahh, there you are, Ash, these people have been looking for you. I told them that you were fine and dandy."* A pitiful, weak smile crossed her face. Ash realised that his mother's condition could have been so much worse, even fatal, had it not been for the protection that had shielded her from the terror and most of the pain she had endured, he was grateful. Ash was then aware of another next to him—he said, "Gran, they have hurt her so badly."

It was then that Ash noticed a new fresh wound on his mother's upper body, a deep black smouldering wound. "No," Ash whispered, realising that the demon general had connected with his mother just before they left and that the injury was fatal. "No," Ash repeated, tears flowing down his face. His gran said in a kind and warm tone, "Ash, there was nothing more you could have done. My daughter will come with me now, and she will have peace. You have done well, Ash." Then his gran took her daughter's hand, and they both faded away before vanishing. The young girl also vanished.

Now alone in his safe place, Ash felt the anger and sadness lift. It was replaced by relief. He was grateful that his mother was now at peace and together again with her mother. In the serenity of the room, a soft, caring voice spoke; Ash knew it was Peter.

"This lesson is now complete Ash, you have endured the worst of pain, and you are now fully equipped for the battle that rages. You must return and face those who you escaped. I have renewed confidence in your ability. It would have been so easy for you to have destroyed the gateway. You did not; you dealt with matters appropriately, you saved many more than you know, none more important than your mother. Now return and follow the path that you have been given."

Then the voice was gone. Ash focused on his will, which was most powerful in his safe place. He was recharged. He was ready to return to the underworld. Ash concentrated and focused on the void beneath Tottenham Court Road.

Chapter 12
The Trap

He opened the air in front of him then stepped into the space. Silently he had returned to hell. It seemed as though no time had actually passed. The demon general was still enraged, obliterating minor demons who feared to glance his way, the loss of his prisoners impacted personally. Ash quietly entered one of the cells from where the abducted young people had escaped from. They, by the way, had made good their escape, all of them armed with more knowledge and compassion for their rescuer than when they were abducted, and they immediately started to spread the word.

The word was Ash.

Without a thought, Ash became enveloped within his invisibility shield, his ability even more potent, concealed him from the demon general's inner-sight. He silently moved around this unholy place without difficulty and was able to listen into the conversation. Ash heard plans being drawn up, intentions shared, and of the final goal!

Several hours passed; the demon general began to settle down. He summoned more of his general staff to complete and finalise the plan they had worked on for so long. It was easier for Ash to draw information from the minds of the minor general staff, although in doing so, Ash had to claw his way through the ruthless hatred that dwelt within the foul demon minds, images of the hurt and suffering each one had handed out in order to climb this dark and evil ladder. The higher their position, the more foul and unimaginable the acts performed.

There was a common thread that linked all of the minds—it was just how easy it was to turn humans into inhuman beings. Ash recalled Brian. This series of events was typical, but Ash had no idea and was shocked at the scale of penetration by the legions from Hell into the realm of earthly human existence. Now Ash understood the scale of the war. He saw leaders of whole countries who had given their souls for their own gratification, their own personal desires. He saw captains of industry, bankers who were securing for themselves wealth and riches at the expense of others. He saw others including celebrities, priests, teachers and politicians whose unholy desire was to indulge in abuse and hurt all manner of people, including the innocence of children. These humans would eventually feed the demon who had assisted them in the first place. Their filthy souls were a rich source for the demon diet. They would also facilitate the demons' rise within the devil's ranks.

Ash needed to look into the mind of the general himself. This foulest creature held clearer and more concise information. It was, however, a very dangerous move. He moved stealthily, cautiously, his mind reached out almost undetectable. Terrors on a massive scale resided in this black mind, evil ambition fuelled its hunger, deviousness, and betrayal underpinning its desire. Looking deeper into this abominable mind, he found his way blocked. He moved more carefully. It seemed that every avenue was blocked, the mind he was in closed around him. He stopped and immediately assessed the situation. To his horror, the full realisation of his situation smashed into the front of his mind. A trap!

Chapter 13
Demon Lord Raths

The connection Ash had made was violently severed, and he was sent hurtling out of control across the slimy floor.

He unceremoniously stopped against a damp, blackened wall. He immediately ignited his inner-defensive force, for the moment, he was safe. At the same time, he heard the terrible booming voice of the demon general Lord Raths, "Oh yes, I was expecting you! You dare to look into my mind, you believe that you are so powerful. Then receive the full power a demon general possesses." As he spoke, Ash felt the general gather its considerable will releasing it as it was gathered. A black force smashed into Ash full-on, he attempted to defend and repel the energy bolt, but there was no defensive move he could make. At the same moment, Ash was completely entombed in a dreadful sizzling energy bubble, a force that Ash had never before encountered. Ash was lifted off his feet. He hung in the foul-smelling air, the charged energy attacking him, smoke emitted from now open raw burns on his body, helpless and in pain, he attempted to force his prison to collapse, but his considerable efforts were futile. The demon said mockingly, "Yes, why not try to escape you poor irritation? Use all that you possess; you are nothing in my realm. Oh dear, you weren't instructed on that matter—the deeper you travel into my realm, the weaker you become. It is quite simple. You are pathetic!"

The demon forced his will at Ash again. Even with

his skill, Ash could not deflect the agonising lashes of hatred that assaulted him. Tearing flashes of ruthless energy ripped at his flesh, deep lacerations appeared on his stricken now naked body. The general's face contorted into pure hatred as he unleashed another bout of agonising energy at Ash.

He hissed, "Did you seriously believe that I would let you know our plan then let you attempt to prevent it? I was aware you were delving into these weak creatures!" The general looked around at the twenty or so staff demons around him, a look of abject contempt on his face. He said, "They are mine. They belong to me. What they know I know, what they do; I instruct, and when they are violated, I know, they do not, I do. Although I must applaud your skill at getting through the protective shield. However, it is clear that they have been careless."

His final words delivered in a scathing and dangerous tone. He was looking intently at the gathered minor demons. A distasteful look flashed across his angry face as he pointed a gnarled bony finger at the nearest demon and said to her, "And you are the weakest of all!" The general raised his hand higher in the air, his face contorted in focus as he looked directly into the face of his failed minion. She attempted to move but was frozen to the spot where she stood.

Her face twisted in agony, a panicked screeching gurgle exploded from the demons gaping mouth, as smouldering green flames spewed out of its eye sockets, her long blonde hair combusted, violently trembling where it stood in front of its Master. She attempted to plead, the general refocused his will at the victim, a vile smirk of satisfaction crossed his features before he released his full might, the minor demon let out one more intense shrill scream before melting into a pool of thick steaming black slime. The general regained a semblance of control and said in a soft patronising tone, "Let that be a lesson to you all."

He turned his attention once again to Ash and snarled, "As we speak, whole legions of my Master's army ready themselves for our final move to eradicate the worthless human race. My Master conceived our plan many eons ago and it will not be stopped by you! What my Master wants he gets, oh, yes, by the way, he is on his way as we have this cosy little chat, he will have the 'Chosen One's' soul for himself, and this time he will be victorious." His voice raising up several tones as he delivered his statement.

The demon roared with hideous laughter, mocking Ash, and sent more pulses of energy bolts at him. Ragged lightning bolts continued to smash into the suspended body of Ash. He was all but defenceless. He was able to withstand the abject pain, but it was drawing his strength quickly. He felt alone, abandoned; for the first time in many years, he felt fear begin to rise within him. The demon general then said in mocking sympathy, "Oh, yes, I sense your fear, you're weakness, your loneliness. And now I will relish in your fear as you receive your reward for being the 'Chosen One'! His voice spitting and booming at this point, and each energy bolt that assaulted Ash, the demon general, twisted its sinister smile more grotesquely. He was in ecstasy.

Chapter 14
Son of Greed

E very part of the interior in the unholy place suddenly vibrated violently as a huge crack appeared on the floor—several of those standing nearest floundering to stand upright. Sulphurous fumes filled the air as filthy dark yellow vapour poured out of the void. Black living slime escaped from the crack, spilling onto the surface of the hell space, it withered and pulsated, the voices of millions of victims screeched in an unholy chorus. The crack widened; green flashes of flame licked at the high roof, scorching several of the closest minions. They shrieked in pain as body parts melted, pouring into the abyss.

The crack in the ground continued to widen. Green flames belched out of the ground, then a parade of demon soldiers marched in a dishevelled line out of the huge crack, each carried what appeared to be a human bone spear mounted with various skulls, animal, bird, and human. They were almost human-like but instead of arms they had insect articulated limbs with claws for hands. Their faces were contorted and under the skin-like covering was movement, as if looking into deep bubbling oil. These soldiers were followed by more ranking soldiers. The pageant continued for some time; then more demon generals entered the large space. All of the demons stood in untidy ranks, all of them twitching, eyeing up their peers, looking for ways to impress their immediate superior in any way possible.

The flames abated, and an unholy silence descended within the void. All present looked into the now vast hole as the final demon appeared. There was no real form, although it resembled human. To the surprise of Ash, who for the time being was not being assaulted with pulse after pulse of evil energy, had been observing from his living cell of hatred energy, the thing that had appeared was tiny, although slightly humanoid. It was almost a childlike being with a huge misshapen head, Ash felt its overwhelming presence. He had never felt such powerful evil before, and he knew that it was he who was the prize!

A demon of huge grotesque bodily proportions levitated above the gathered army, sparks of energy ignited around its great bulk as it ascended and in a deep guttural voice, it announced the arrival of the demon overlord, it uttered, "Behold, our Master, the slayer of the Chosen One, the Son of Greed, for he has arisen once more to complete what began before time itself". There was a roar from the massive assembly. He continued, "Our Master will pave the way for us to dominate the human race, to control the weakness of mankind, to take what is rightly his to take. To consume every human soul"

There was another huge roar of excited grotesque agreement. "But first, the simple matter of revenge for the suffering inflicted on our Master by those who would care for and protect these insignificant mortal, weak creatures. Take him!" ordered the general to several soldier demons who were guarding the energy sphere imprisoning Ash.

Chapter 15
Into Hell

Between them, the soldiers combined their will and moved the cell towards the huge crack. Ash looked wide-eyed as he was carried to the edge of Hell itself. Every fibre within him began to fight, every atom that made Ash screamed in agony, all remained contained within the powerful imprisonment sphere. Slowly Ash was moved down into the green fire pit. There was silence apart from the fidgeting sound of demons twitching. The Son of Greed stealthily followed at a distance. His tiny body was glowing with a deep redness, flashes of charged particles erupted all around him, in his wake, thick black smoke hung in the foul air. As Ash was carried to the entrance, the procession stopped. In a dreadful voice the son of Greed pronounced, in a hissing tone, "At last, I will do what my father failed to do. I will have the Chosen One, he will be mine forever."

Ash was moved deeper and deeper into the gaping void, passing through areas of defensive shimmering evil energy. Ash knew that this was protection from the outside world — even Hell feels intimidated! As he and the procession continued, Ash could hear the terrified howling of those souls that had been assimilated into the fibre of Hell. The rank smell of sulphur filled the space, black and red slime pulsated on every surface, and vile chaos was everywhere.

It was odd he thought, even though he was severely injured and within this hellish environment, he knew that a part of him was not being effected by any of the evil surrounding him, he was simply passing through, to where was not clear and the onward journey was less clear. He looked curiously through into the inner-sanctum of Hell, there he noted another type of altar, it convulsed like a beating heart, barely a life form, but it was able to hold its form as an altar. Ash knew that this was for him, this thought was almost casual, he knew that he was to be sacrificed but much worse Ash realised that he would be consumed by the overlord, once again this thought was almost as casual as the previous thought.

The demon soldiers dropped Ash's prison onto the altar. Dark claw-like talons appeared from within the living altar. They sunk the spindly talons into the cocoon and secured it in place. There was no escape; the sacrifice was set to take place.

Even though it was clear that he was in immediate peril Ash released his fear. As his fear had strengthened the invisible force that contained him, Ash started to breathe more slowly, his heart calmed, and he started a controlled retreat into himself. He calmed his inner-self and became at peace and at that moment gave himself to whatever horror was about to take place. This was the way it was meant to be. He was content. The cocoon surrounding Ash began to flicker, the fear with which it gathered energy was no longer available, the talons holding onto the energy field began to grapple for purchase, the energy continued to fail. Several of the closest demons fidgeted more noticeably, unsure of how to respond to the failing forcefield.

Inside Hell everything stopped. A hideous silence much louder than the crazy noise of Hell brought all to a semblance of order, apart from most of the demons who continued their uncontrollable twitching. Hell's overlord, the Son of Greed approached the altar. Despite its small form, the voice it spoke with from its huge bulbous head was peculiar. He said in a vibrato tone, "I have waited ever since my father was spread across the universes, waited for the time you would arrive, time for my plan to be put into action, time for my ultimate desire to be fulfilled." He paused and focused his tiny eyes directly on the face of Ash. He was able to look directly into Ash's soul. The overlord continued in a dangerous quieter tone, "And now the waiting is over. The time has arrived for me to own this wretched planet, time for my influence to reign supreme, and now Chosen One, know my hatred for you, taste what will be your existence for the rest of time. You are mine!" The hatred in his voice rose louder and louder until it boomed and travelled like a thunderclap through the planet. Several thousand miles away, the force of intent ignited a dormant volcano. It erupted spontaneously, throwing green sulphurous gas into the air, it began to spread.

The Overlord placed his tiny hand-like claws onto the altar; they seemed to melt into the seething mass of movement. At the same moment, the black pulsating slime began to climb around the energy cocoon. As it climbed, a look of outrageous joy filled the face of the Overlord. Swaying from side to side, almost cooing in delight, he sunk his claws deeper into the slime. At the same time, Ash's cell was being consumed by the entity. Then the Overlord blended with the black living slime, which straight away was filled with a hatred even those present had never encountered—some of the demons even winced in fear.

Inside of his prison cell, Ash watched as the dim light around him was plunged into darkness. The skills he had gathered were crushed by the intensity of evil presented by his ultimate captor. He could feel his flesh was being absorbed into the slime. He saw and felt the evil hatred and contempt for his existence; he saw what the Overlord saw. He closed his eyes. Time was standing still in Hell while on the surface of the earth it raced by.

A roar of hideous proportions echoed through Hell. The Overlord had beaten his ultimate adversary, which was forever contained within itself. Then in a dreadful tone, it said, "Now it is time for the planet to bow to me!"

Chapter 16
The Few

Another dormant volcano, this time in America, erupted violently. It ejected billions of tons of green ash. And much more, this was no ordinary volcanic event, this volcano had its roots in hell. Together with the ash there were demented souls of thousands of victims of demon attacks. All with one single goal—to claim a soul for themselves. Hell was unleashed on earth. The ash travelled higher into the atmosphere where the jet stream very quickly carried the thick dust around the planet. Within twenty-four hours, the light from the sun was hidden from the surface of the Earth. Coldness spread to every space, flowers and crops began to wilt, freshwater became poisoned by the fallout from the volcano. The Overlord smiled with satisfaction.

Panic began, looting of shops, stealing from the vulnerable. From their penthouse suites, many men and women looked around at the civil unrest, smiling and applauding themselves inwardly, for this is what they had been promised—domination of the many by the few! What they had not foreseen was what was about to arrive on the surface.

For a time it would seem to the few that the entire wealth of the planet was going to be owned by the tiniest percentage of the human race, all of whom had made a deal with Hell. The rest of civilisation would belong to them. This thought was of course flawed as all would become the property of and under the dominion of the Overlord of Hell.

Chapter 17
Ash Ash

In a modest detached house in the Highlands of Scotland, a family with friends and neighbours were sitting around the dining table. Life was good, and all were quite content until the skies began to darken and the cold arrived.

Jane, a mother of the two children, had invited neighbours into her home for warmth and shelter. She offered a portion of home-grown vegetables to her guests and loving husband. They all accepted the smaller than usual offerings, and were grateful for the food as well as a warmer friendly environment they now shared with this family.

They all sat down at the table again. The quiet chattering stopped as Jane quite suddenly lifted her face upward and began to stare into the air. It seemed that she was in some sort of catatonic state, her eyes wide and staring. Her husband and children, along with the other houseguests, looked at her in surprise. Huge tears suddenly filled the corner of her eyes and ran down her face; she said in a quiet voice, "His name was Ash, it was him, Ash!" Instantly the children said together, "I remember him, mummy, he was that nice man who visited us, but I have only just remembered him." Jane said to her husband, "It was Ash, such a wonderful man."

Then her husband said, "Yes, I know, I have always known of him but never thought about him and his kindness and the offering of hope he gave to us as a family." Then one of the houseguests said, "Ash, Ash." A look of surprise appeared on the guest's face because for no reason, she was now aware of a person whose name was Ash, and she knew he was good.

The family still sitting at the table recounted the visit they had had from Ash and remembered what he had done and left with them.

"Ash, Ash, Ash, thank you, we love you." Repeating over and over, joy and love in the voices.

Throughout the Highlands, in hundreds of homes, hospitals, schools, and offices, at the same moment, the memory of Ash was remembered. All began to say the words 'Ash, Ash'. All knew that he was a good man that had given them hope.

Word rapidly began to spread about a person called Ash, the 'lovely man' who had helped and given hope to so many people. Even as the skies above them continued to darken, and as the temperature quickly became much colder, hundreds of people spoke the words, "Ash, Ash." At the sound of this name, several minor demons who had escaped from hell via the volcano suddenly shimmered and vanished.

People of all faiths and those with no faith went to their nearest church or chapel or gathering places. Public parks filled with men, women and children of all ages, all possessed with the same knowledge—that a young man whose name was Ash had done acts of unbelievable kindness, relieved suffering, comforted those in need, but most of all gave hope. And now was in mortal danger. Word spread wider and wider. Ash, Ash. A group of young people who had been rescued from a certain horrific death, found themselves remembering more details, and how it was Ash who had given them the ability to escape from the damp cells at the bottom of Gooch Street tube station. They passed on the words, 'Ash, Ash.' They also shared in what had been given to them—'hope'. Suddenly in their despair and in the dim cold of the new environment, the population of the UK began to call in unison the same two words,' Ash, Ash'. They also felt intense hope.

In the areas where civil unrest had started, suddenly and spontaneously, people started saying the two words,' Ash, Ash'. And they too sensed 'hope'. 'Hope' began to replace dread in the front of minds of ordinary people, slowly at first, but picking up momentum and soon the feeling of 'HOPE' became tangible, people could all but hold it in their hearts.

In their penthouse-offices, those who had smirked at their apparent great fortune and applauded as the darkness began to consume the light, started to take notice of the mood and positivity of the people around them.

Even those who had been sacked or abused by the new regime started to gather in themselves new hope. The two words that seemed to be generating this hope were, 'Ash, Ash". The initial euphoric excitement exhibited by the 'soul sellers' was now beginning to be replaced by an uncomfortable thought that not all was right, that they were in some sort of danger, a danger that could not have been foreseen, as dread entered their souls they began to twitch.

Chapter 18
Final Plans

As the Demon generals continued to make their final plans to ascend from Hell and occupy the new dark world, several of them received reports of another threat, a threat that was building on the surface.

With overwhelming arrogance and complete denial, the senior demons simply dismissed this threat, believing that, 'nothing can prevent us now', and so they continued with their unholy planning.

Chapter 19
Raised Voices

Across the English Channel and spreading through the North and South of France, the words continued to spread, "Ash, Ash". Everyone who spoke the two simple words understood and felt that what it meant, 'hope' was with them even while the darkness consumed all light.

The words spread through Italy; His Holiness the Pope understood immediately the significance of the words. He instructed, "In these dark times, we must focus on the two words that have been sent to us. We must accept 'hope' and know that one day the darkness will again be light". "Ash, Ash," he said.

Within days a billion voices were calling with one voice, "Ash, Ash".

Chapter 20
Revenge

The words spread across the great continents, even where language is so very different, the words were spoken, and so on the tenth day, every corner of the planet Earth was speaking with one voice, "Ash, Ash".

Two billion voices — "Ash, Ash".

The significance of what was occurring on the surface of Earth began to filter into the depths of Hell, carried by frantic worshippers of evil, fleeing the vulgar opulence of their offices, abandoning their badges of honour, with hands attempting to shield their ears from the words which they had begun to fear. The words caused them pain, and the only escape was to find their way into Hell, by any means, Abandoning all of their apparent privileges and wealth.

Three billion voices — "Ash, Ash".

Chapter 21
Revenge II

Deep in the bowels of Hell, soldier demons realising that there was a large influx of their servants, began to kill them and consume what was remaining of the individual's soul. With abject contempt for the information which was arriving in the lower levels of Hell, the ranks of demons simply deflected any suggestion that their plans may be thwarted. One demon general obliterated a whole regiment of soldier demons for even thinking that there were any issues.

Four Billion voices—"Ash, Ash".

In the very centre of Hell, where protection from all else was most potent and deaf to all else but their thoughts, the Overlord and his most senior demon Lords were about to begin the journey to the surface where the final acts of brutality and abuse for those who refused to follow were going to take place.

This was to be the birth of the 'new dark age', the age of 'Darkness of revenge', where there would be only one entity who would be obeyed, where it would feed off the suffering of mankind, where breeding programs would produce fine young fresh souls to be devoured. Where no light would exist apart from the glow of green sulphurous gas.

Five Billion voices—"Ash, Ash". Six Billion voices—"Ash, Ash".

The sense of 'hope' intensified around the globe. A tangible force that began to dissipate the darkness and the scavenging demon souls. As the Overlord of Hell took his place at the head of his army on top of the steps in the centre of his brutal environment, a pulse of energy shook the entire foundations. The energy stopped the Overlord in his tracks. Then there was another gigantic pulse of energy. Many of the soldiers stumbled as if the whole of Hell had suffered a massive earthquake. Looks and murmurs of shock began to fill the huge space. Panicking demons looked at each other. Their twitching intensified as questions were muttered, "What is happening?"

Chapter 22
The Chorus

In every village and town, in every community, in every country, on every continent on the planet Earth and at the same moment both day and night, with one voice the two words rang out. *"ASH, ASH!"* The glorious sound was global, the energy generated by the combined voices of mankind consumed the entire planet. Within the words was a clear message— *Hope.*

The chorus of seven billion voices joined as one. The sound travelled through all barriers with ease, smashing through the toughest barrier into the core of Hell. Nothing prevented its pure momentum, where resistance stood, it was washed away in the torrent of humanitarian solidarity .

Then, finding its target, the sound focused, condensing, consolidating, strengthening, pinpointing into the size of an atom, before striking at its target.

Hell's Overlord, the Son of Greed stood quite still, almost statue-like at the head of its legions. It was aware of the overwhelming force that had just penetrated its domain. The Overlord looked at its generals, confusion on its features, like a child being told off and not understanding the reason for it.

The generals, for the first time in their existence, sensed fear. It was a taste so bitter and strong that they attempted to focus their will on protecting themselves from this force. Knowing that these demons were attempting to protect themselves and not their Overlord, with a gesture from the Son of Greed, the offending demons exploded into black, red slime. The Overlord hissed, "Anyone else?"

Chapter 23
The Atom

In the core of Hell, an atom containing the will of the billions of men, women, and children moved around the space then stopped in front of the Overlord. With tiny claws, the Overlord took the atom and gave it a strange confused look and said in a quiet voice, "And what do we have here I wonder, how did you arrive in my domain?"

The atom simply freed itself from between the claw-like hand of the Overlord. It hung like a single bright star in the dark, putrid air in front of its target; then the atom began to spin, picking up momentum becoming brighter as it did so, selecting the exact point, the light from the atom grew and grew, it's light on contact with the other demons melted them where they stood. Then spinning, it flew directly at the grotesque head of the demon. The atom smashed directly into the skull and drove itself into the consciousness of the Son of Greed. A look of complete outrage and hatred crossed the demon's features as it stood dumbstruck and motionless. All light within Hell suddenly went out, leaving the dull green glow.

Deep within the Overlords consciousness at the point of contact between the atom and the target, a spark ignited, the joining of the two created a tiny ripple effect. On the crest of each ripple wave, another spark ignited, then another pulse and ripple, then more sparks. Where the joining of the atom and the first spark had taken place grew a tiny light, the light became more intense.

Chapter 24
Incandescent Light II

The Overlord of Hell twitched. The inside of his tiny body began to vibrate as with each passing microsecond, flashes and ripples travelled from within his consciousness. Observing what was taking place, the demon generals started to move away from their Master, only to find that their forward motion was being barred. They were being held close to the Overlord by his will. The Overlord began to take energy from his generals, attempting to extinguish the flashes of energy igniting within its fibres.

Inside the demon's consciousness, momentum continued to grow. Flashes of pure energy followed by more powerful waves travelled further through the host. The Overlord of Hell forced his will to attack the light within him. It was useless. From within the centre of Hell, a chorus of voices could be heard, soft at first but getting louder by the second—"Ash, Ash." Following this, the alien concept of hope began to filter into Hell. The combination of the two produced a violent reaction from the gathered demon army. Many of the soldiers simply trembled and melted on the spot; others covered their ears with claws. This of course, was of little help as the voices and feeling of hope just became bigger, engulfing them.

After a minute or so, the Overlord looked up from where he stood and in a monstrous cry shouted, "No, what have you done?" Within the demon Overlord, the chain reaction increased in speed. It was travelling and destroying every fibre within the evil matter. Then with a tiny voice, the demon overlord hissed, "Father, help me!"

With that, the Overlord melted into a mass of writhing black-red slime, followed by his generals, then all of the legions began to melt. The screams of agony rang through Hell, but not one of the demons escaped.

From within the decaying black slime, a light began to rise to the surface. It broke free of the unholy mass, then became incandescent blue and launched itself out of Hell, leaving behind a melted mass of slowly solidifying black slime. As the light left Hell, the whole of this sub-earth realm began to collapse on itself, and within seconds nothing remained.

Chapter 25
Sunlight

A round the world, all who had given their souls to become part of Hell suddenly collapsed and melted into the Earth. No demon survived; Evil was no more on Earth.

As the incandescent globe of light travelled through the planet towards the surface, the Earth shifted on its axis. This movement brought the planet to a brief standstill, then very slowly at first in its new orbit Earth once again began to rotate. The rotation created a new jet stream. The jet stream developed into a tornado. The tornado touched the blackened debris from the volcano, which was hanging in the atmosphere preventing the warmth and light of the Sun getting through.

Swirling at supersonic speed, the jet stream slowly started to remove the volcanic ash, depositing it into space where it travelled away from the planet. Within twelve hours across Europe, sunlight once again touched the faces of the millions of people who were still standing and saying the same two words, *"Ash, Ash"*.

Sunlight quickly warmed up the surface of the planet, and where there had been vast areas of the surface that were barren and dried out, rain clouds developed over them, then quenched the ground. Seeds that had laid dormant for decades suddenly burst into life. Green replaced brown. The waters purified themselves and where there had not been any water, now springs appeared. The planet Earth was healing herself. She was breathing new fresh air. In a small community in the Highlands of Scotland, a family and newly-found friends looked into the skies, and the mother of two children said, "We did it, we really did it." Her husband said, "Yes, Jane, we did."

Chapter 26
Special Place

Sitting at a table in the 'Safe Place' was a woman. She had the brightest violet eyes and iridescent blue- white hair. There were three men also sitting around the table quietly talking. In front of them were crystal glasses containing pure water; there were also two other chairs and two glasses containing pure water.

While deep in conversation, a door that had not previously been there opened. Stepping into the safe place, Ash walked in. He nodded with the deepest respect at the woman who responded with loving respect, then Ash acknowledged the other men respectfully. They did the same, then one of the men spoke, "Ash, welcome, I am sure that you have questions, which will be answered."

Then the woman said, "Dear Ash, please take a seat at my table." Ash sat and instinctively took a deep drink from the glass in front of him. She continued, "Ash, from this moment, you are and will forever be remembered as hope. What you gave to the planet Earth was such a powerful gift, the gift of hope. For countless years you shared with man what they would eventually need."

Ash replied, "But I simply followed instructions." Peter replied, "What you received was knowledge, and it was up to you how you used it. Ash, you have done well." Then the woman said: "We realised far too late that the Son of Greed had come of age. Yes, we could have intervened, but the cost to this precious planet would have been too much as we realised an age ago. We would not have been able to enter his realm, for to do so would have informed him of our intention. The Son of Greed was very powerful, and in his realm he was too powerful. That is why when you were made a prisoner and contained within your cocoon your purpose could be shielded as you were taken into the very core of Hell's realm. For only in there were you able to undo what had been created over the ages."

Ash said, "What has become of the Overlord?" Peter replied, "He is no more, the seed is destroyed." The woman then said: "Never again will this beautiful planet suffer, never again will any entity have domination over her or hold her people hostage. The entire population has suffered enough. They made a brave decision through you, Ash, and they deserve peace. I will give protection to this special planet; it will allow the human race to develop into a peaceful world with no hunger or needs. They will know love, compassion and will always have hope. Until the Sun fades, the planet Earth will be the 'Chosen Planet'".

The woman then stood up and concentrated. She said, "It is done." Extending her arms to the four around the table she said, "Our time in this part of the Universes is complete; we must seek the other 'Chosen Planets' and ensure that Greed has not been able to corrupt them. Ash, you will go with Peter." She then turned away and faded into the whiteness of the 'Safe Place'. Peter turned to Ash and said, "And so brother, we continue together, come." They both faded into the whiteness. The safe place also vanished.

Chapter 27
The Young Man of Hope

From the surface of the Earth during the day, the population of Earth could see faded multi-coloured soft flashes in the sky. At night the full colours of the 'protection' of the planet were intense and beautiful, as if a perpetual Aurora Borealis surrounded the planet.

On the ground, crops continued to grow where there had only been dust; fresh sweet water rose from within the Earth, refreshing all on the planet. No longer was the planet plundered for wealth and desire. Peace and harmony swiftly took hold.

In the Highlands of Scotland, a metallic green tin whistle began to play. This was joined by the strings of a bazuki. This instrument was recycled from an old chest of drawers. They were joined by a fiddle. As the music started, the sound spread through the Glens, through the mountains, along the rivers and lochs. The tune was a simple but beautiful set, with the title *'The Young Man of Hope'*. As the beautiful music filled the landscape, people looked skywards and watched as the sky moved to the rhythms. Mankind was forever at peace.

In a universe, billions of light-years away from this universe, gradually growing and getting stronger, was a small mass of black slime. The slime stopped shimmering briefly as reaching it from another time and space were the words, *"Father, help me!"*

Lightning Source UK Ltd.
Milton Keynes UK
UKHW041826201221
395980UK00001B/1

9 781739 825829